"I managed perfectly well before you came along!"

Dark brows rose mockingly at her statement. "Does that mean you're having some difficulty doing so now?" he challenged softly.

"Certainly not!" She snapped her resentment. He was being deliberately provocative, but he could have no idea of the full reason his taunts were so successful. She drew in a ragged breath. "I appreciate your help—"

"Little liar!" He laughed softly at her obvious discomfort with having to thank him for anything. "But you will," he added gruffly. "Thank me, I mean."

"Mortimer has a special magic."
—*Romantic Times*

CAROLE MORTIMER, one of our most popular—and prolific—English authors, began writing in the Harlequin Presents series in 1979. She writes strong traditional romances with a distinctly modern appeal, and her winning way with characters and romantic plot twists has earned her an enthusiastic audience worldwide. Carole Mortimer lives on the Isle of Man with her family and menagerie of pets. She claims this busy household has helped to inspire her writing.

Books by Carole Mortimer

HARLEQUIN PRESENTS PLUS
1559—THE JILTED BRIDEGROOM

HARLEQUIN PRESENTS
1258—ELUSIVE AS THE UNICORN
1325—A CHRISTMAS AFFAIR
1451—MEMORIES OF THE PAST
1468—ROMANCE OF A LIFETIME
1543—SAVING GRACE

Don't miss any of our special offers. Write to us at the following address for information on our newest releases.

Harlequin Reader Service
P.O. Box 1397, Buffalo, NY 14240
Canadian address: P.O. Box 603,
Fort Erie, Ont. L2A 5X3

Carole Mortimer

PRIVATE Lives

Harlequin Books

TORONTO • NEW YORK • LONDON
AMSTERDAM • PARIS • SYDNEY • HAMBURG
STOCKHOLM • ATHENS • TOKYO • MILAN
MADRID • WARSAW • BUDAPEST • AUCKLAND

For
Matthew, Joshua, and Timothy

Harlequin Presents Plus first edition September 1993
ISBN 0-373-11583-0

Original hardcover edition published in 1992
by Mills & Boon Limited

PRIVATE LIVES

CHAPTER ONE

'THERE'S a man in the bed!'

It was too early in the morning to be listening to fairy-tales!

'Fin, there's a man in the bed!' The voice on the other end of the telephone line was more urgent this time.

And it was *far* too early in the morning for obscene telephone calls!

'Fin, I know you're there, listening to this, because that stupid machine hasn't come on, so for God's sake answer me!' The voice was no more than a hoarse whisper down the line, but nevertheless the panic in the tone seemed to be increasing. 'Do you think I should call the police?'

Fin had been listening to the tape of received messages that 'that stupid machine' had made since she closed the office for business the evening before, but at the mention of the police she turned her full attention back to the telephone conversation in hand. 'Ella, is that you?' she frowned.

'Of course it's——' The other woman broke off abruptly, drawing in deep controlling breaths as she realised she had raised her voice in her agitation. 'Of course it's me!' she confirmed almost desperately, her voice low again. 'I'm at Gail's cottage, doing my usual check, and *there's a man in the bed*!'

Fin couldn't help smiling at this repetition of those words. 'Then lock the door behind you and leave them to it!' she advised with indulgence. She had seen and done a lot of unusual things the last two years since she had set up in business, walked unwittingly into all sorts of embarrassing situations, and finding one of their clients in bed with her boyfriend was the least of them!

She hadn't been sure her idea would work out when she had first bought a decrepit old van, painted it bright colours, daubed a catchy name on the side, and advertised herself as a sort of 'Girl Friday', no job too big or too small, too difficult or too trivial. She wasn't so sure that that had ever been strictly true, but she had always done her best to find someone else who could do the job if it really was out of her sphere to do it properly.

During the first year she had done everything required herself, from walking a Siamese cat on a lead for its owner because he felt too ridiculous doing it himself, to collecting children from school for busy parents, to keeping watch over people's homes for them while they were away, as they were doing at Rose Cottage now for Gail Moore.

The business had expanded in the last year, so that now she had two part-time assistants working for her too: a school-leaver who didn't want to go into a routine office job—this work could never be called routine!—and Ella, a woman in her fifties, bored with being a housewife with her husband out at work all day and her children all having left home by now, either because they had married, or gone on to further education that required them to live near their university.

Ella's first job of this morning had been to check on Rose Cottage while Gail was away in London, working, during the week. Obviously Gail had come back early—with a friend!—and forgotten to let them know not to call in this morning. Poor Ella sounded devastated!

'You don't understand, Fin,' Ella came back exasperatedly now. 'Gail isn't here; he's alone in the bed!'

That did put a slightly different light on things. 'Have you checked—of course you have,' she answered her own question as she realised she was only adding fuel to the fire. 'Maybe Gail invited a friend down to use the cottage while she's away and just forgot to mention it to us.' She frowned, chewing on the end of the pencil she had picked up when the call first came through, having expected it to be someone requesting her home-help services rather than this! 'Why don't you ask him?' she suggested gently, wondering why Ella hadn't already done that. She soon got her answer!

'Because he's *drunk*!' her employee announced disgustedly. 'The bedroom stinks of whisky! And there's an empty bottle and glass lying beside the bed,' she added triumphantly, as if to show she hadn't drawn her conclusion as to the man's condition without due cause.

Even so, calling in the police did seem a little extreme in the circumstances. If this man actually was a friend of Gail's the other woman wasn't going to be too pleased if they had him arrested!

'Look, I——' Fin broke off with a dismayed groan as one of the messages she had been half-heartedly listening to hit her like a bombshell; this was all she needed! 'I'll be out to the cottage myself as soon as I can get there, Ella,' she told the other woman distractedly.

'I can't just go away and leave him here,' the older woman protested, scandalised at the very idea.

'No, I—of course not,' Fin accepted, hoping that she had misheard the message on the tape. 'Go outside, Ella, and—and wait on your bicycle,' she advised vaguely before ringing off, removing her hand from the receiver as if it were red-hot as she realised that she had just literally told the poor woman to 'get on her bike'! What must poor Ella think of her?

It had been that particular message left on the answer-machine that had so unnerved her, of course, and she frowned as she rewound it, ready to play it back again, giving *it* her full attention now.

'I tried your home number earlier and there was no reply,' came the slightly reproving voice of the secretary of the amateur dramatics group Fin belonged to. 'We have a catastrophe on our hands, darling,' Delia continued heavily. 'Gerald Dunn has thrown a wobbler and withdrawn from the production as our director! It's just too bad of him at this stage of the proceedings,' she complained waspishly. 'But it means we shall have to call an emergency committee meeting Wednesday night—that's tomorrow—to try and pull the thing back together. As a committee member, you have to be there, Fin.' Again that autocratic edge entered the other woman's voice. 'Eight o'clock sharp, at my house.' The message ended abruptly.

There had been no mistake; that was exactly what Fin had thought the message contained the first time she heard it!

There had been no one at home to take the call the previous evening because she had been out with Derek, and her mother and stepfather had been invited out to a dinner party.

And Derek wasn't going to be at all pleased about the emergency committee meeting being called for tonight. Fin had been cast in the group's latest play, and tonight had supposedly been one of the precious nights off from rehearsal for her, and Derek had intended taking her out for a meal. It would be no good suggesting they still go out for the meal after the meeting either, because if Gerald really had withdrawn from the play then they could be talking for hours about finding his replacement.

Just over three weeks before the play was due to go on at the local theatre and they had no director!

Fin had known Gerald wasn't happy the last few weeks, having recently changed his job and feeling the strain of the uncertainty of that with a wife and baby at home to support; the added pressure of the responsibility for directing the play was obviously too much for him. And who could really blame him? Actually, they should all respect him for the fact that he wasn't too proud to stand up and say he had made a mistake in taking on the job in the first place! It didn't put the rest of the cast in a very good position, but at least it was honest.

Fin had begun to wish herself that she had never got involved with the production—*Private*

Lives, one of Noël Coward's highly entertaining dry-wit comedies; but, as Derek had complained repeatedly the last few weeks when she had been required to spend at least two, sometimes three evenings a week at the local village hall, rehearsing, a private life was something *they* didn't have at the moment, and wouldn't have until the play was over. She hardly dared tell him that as from next week those rehearsal nights increased to five nights a week *and* Sunday afternoons!

But at the moment Fin had something much more pressing to deal with than either Derek or the difficulties with the play; poor Ella was still 'on her bike' outside Rose Cottage, with a drunken stranger prostrate on the bed upstairs!

She switched on the answer-machine again and hurried out to the van parked outside, a new van now that business was so successful, much more reliable for getting around in, the old one having had a tendency to break down at the most inconvenient moments. Not that she managed to get out on jobs herself as much as she used to, finding that she was spending more and more time at the tiny office she rented in town, doing tedious paperwork that Derek, as her accountant, assured her had to be done for the efficient running of the business. Although she still had the dubious honour of walking the Siamese cat daily, its owner refusing to trust anyone else with it!

And so the unexpected trip out this morning, when she had thought it would be yet another two or three hours stuck behind her desk, was something of a treat for her. As long as she didn't have to deal with a violent drunk once she got to the cottage!

Ella sat on the grey stone wall outside the picturesque cottage in this little Bedfordshire hamlet, although her bicycle was propped up against the wall beside her, just in case of a quick getaway being necessary, Fin guessed wryly.

The cottage looked peaceful enough from the outside; in fact, it looked lovely in the early-June sunshine, with a lot of the flowers in the garden in bloom, a wild rose trailing above the arched doorway and pretty pink roses blooming there; Fin couldn't really take seriously the possibility that at any minute some drunken homicidal maniac was going to come lurching out of that green-painted door and attack them.

Ella obviously found it a little hard to believe too with hindsight, looking shamefaced as she climbed down off the wall to join Fin as she got out of the van. 'Maybe I should just have woken him and——'

'No, no, you did the right thing in calling me,' Fin told her with a reassuring smile, her short red curls gleaming in the sunshine, a sprinkling of freckles across her nose and cheeks, as she squinted up at the cottage.

She stood barely five feet in height even in her white track-shoes, was as slender as a teenager, and certainly didn't look the twenty-one years she was, with her face bare of make-up and dressed in close-fitting jeans and a white T-shirt with a disparaging remark about mornings printed on its front.

'Don't worry,' she laughed softly as she saw Ella's look of uncertainty at her ability to deal with the 'intruder' with the disadvantage of her diminutive size, 'I've taken a course in self-defence.' It had been necessary when she'd first set up in business; some men had been mistaken about the type of 'services' she provided then, and hadn't been prepared to take no for an answer! That didn't happen very often nowadays, thank goodness, most people in the area knowing exactly what she was prepared to do and what she wasn't. And *that* was one of the things she wasn't!

'I'll come with you anyway,' the older woman offered with a frown.

'It really isn't necessary,' Fin told her with a dismissive laugh, but making no further protests when she saw that Ella was determined to accompany her, trailing behind Fin as she entered the low-beamed kitchen.

Everything looked as neat and tidy as usual in here, no porridge that was 'too hot, too cold, or just right', no chair that was 'too hard, too soft, or just right' either, and so Fin knew she had been right about the fairy-tales. Although she didn't think Ella would appreciate her humour over the matter just now!

And Ella had been right about one thing: there was a man in the bed, Fin discovered when she looked in the nearest of the two bedrooms at the top of the stairs. It was Gail's own bedroom, but there was indeed only one person in the bed. He was spread-eagled across the middle of it, and looked as if he had been so for some time, by the disarray of the duvet.

The room was in shadow, with the curtains drawn across the window, shutting out the bright sunshine, the man in the bed no more than an untidy lump beneath the duvet. A fact, Fin acknowledged with a frown, that must have been very disturbing for Ella when she had first arrived.

The man was big and tall—Fin could tell that much from the amount of space he took up in the bed—and his hair was thick and dark as it lay against the cream-coloured pillow-case. And his breathing was low and even, not quite a snore, as he slept. An alcohol-induced sleep, from the smell of whisky in the room and that empty bottle and glass on the floor, Fin guessed too.

Their entrance to the cottage hadn't disturbed him in the least. And he was equally unaffected by their presence in the bedroom!

If they had had any idea of who he was there might have been something amusing about the situation. Might...

Well, whoever he was, at the very least they were perfectly within their rights to demand an explanation from him for his presence here, Fin decided, crossing the room to pull back the curtains with a determined movement of her hands, sunlight instantly flooding the cheerfully furnished bedroom with its cream and red colour-scheme.

The only reaction from the man in the bed was a disgruntled snort before he rolled over and buried his face in the pillow to shut out the intrusive light.

Fin ruefully raised her brows in Ella's direction as the other woman still stood in the doorway. 'That achieved a lot,' she murmured self-disgustedly, moving to shake the man as he lay burrowed beneath the duvet now. 'Wake up,' she instructed briskly, hoping the tone of her voice would penetrate, at least. When it didn't she shook him again. 'We would like to talk to you.' That 'we' was put in just in case he *could* hear her, the two women at least protection for one another. She hoped!

Another grunt was her only reply, the duvet pulled more firmly about his shoulders.

It was this defensive action that spurred Fin on to her next move. 'Obviously more drastic

measures are needed here!' she told Ella wryly,
reaching out for the bedclothes.

Ella's eyes widened in protest as Fin's meaning
became clear to her. 'Fin, I don't think—— Oh,
dear,' she groaned weakly as Fin wrenched the
duvet away to reveal that the man who lay beneath it was completely naked! 'Oh, dear. Oh,
dear, oh, dear,' Ella gasped breathlessly.

Oh, dear, oh, dear, *oh*, *dear*, indeed!

The man was lying face-down on the bed, but
nevertheless the naked width of his shoulders,
tapered waist, perfectly moulded buttocks, and
long muscular legs, all covered with fine dark
hair, showed that he was a fine specimen of ma-
ture manhood.

And still he didn't move!

'Wow,' Ella breathed softly into the complete
silence that had fallen over the bedroom in the
last few seconds.

Fin looked at Ella. Ella looked back at Fin.
And suddenly they were grinning at each other
like bemused adolescents.

But the grins suddenly turned to alarm as the
man in the bed finally began to move, the sudden chill perhaps, the bright sunshine, obviously
now having made an impression on his numbed
senses. And Fin heard Ella catch her breath anew
as the man rolled over on to his back.

He was beautifully, magnificently male, looked
like Michelangelo's 'David'. And yet Fin's own

gasp was for quite another reason than his male beauty.

Not him! Any other man in the world but him!

It couldn't *be* him, not *here*. This was sleepy Bedfordshire, miles away from London. Although, a mocking little voice inside her head reminded, the trains in this area now ran directly into London, which was the reason Gail had bought the cottage here in the first place!

But it wasn't him. It couldn't be. The longer Fin stared at that harshly hewn face, the more she convinced herself that she had to be mistaken, that there was merely a facial resemblance.

His hair was thick and dark but streaked with grey, over-long, almost down to his shoulders. Long eyelashes rested on cheekbones that looked as if they were carved out of granite, the nose long and straight, perfectly sculptured lips, slightly parted as the deepness of the breathing increased now that he was lying flat on his back, the angle of his chin thrusting and aggressive even in sleep.

He didn't look *quite* the same, Fin decided, the hair more unkempt than she remembered, and this man looked older—of course he looked older, she rebuked herself impatiently; if this was the man she thought it could be then he was *years* older, must be in his late thirties now. But it couldn't *be* him, she tried to convince herself again, at the same time continuing to look down at him with that same initial fascinated horror.

'This doesn't seem quite—fair,' Ella announced firmly, moving to cover the man's nakedness with the duvet, obviously misunderstanding Fin's interest for one of voyeurism!

When it wasn't this man's nakedness—magnificent as that might be!—that held her enthralled, but the terrible sense of familiarity that just looking at this man gave her...!

But before she could make any attempt to defend her interest to the other woman the man in the bed finally began to stir, Ella stepping back from the bed almost guiltily now, leaving Fin in his direct line of vision as the man's lids were raised above the most incredible pair of aquamarine-coloured eyes she had ever seen! Thick dark lashes added to the incredible depths of that colour, a dark ring of blue encircling the iris to add to their uniqueness, the gaze so piercing, even on waking, that Fin felt pinned to the spot. She was the one who had a perfect right to be here, and yet she felt like fleeing—at the same time knowing she couldn't have moved if she had tried!

He blinked up at her for several seconds, frowning darkly, obviously aware, somewhere at the back of his mind, that she shouldn't be here, that she definitely hadn't been when he'd fallen

asleep. He didn't seem to have seen poor Ella at
all as she stood at the back of the room near the
door, concentrating on Fin with effort. 'Who are
you?' he asked gruffly, as if just the effort of
talking hurt the dryness of his throat.

Now they were back to the original fairy-tale,
only this one didn't seem to be running true to
form at all; wasn't *she* supposed to be the one
asking the questions? And there was such a lot
she would have liked to ask...! 'I'm one of the
Little People——'

'Oh, my God...!' He gave a pained groan, his
pallor increasing, his cheeks looking grey now.
'Oh, *God*!' he groaned again, his eyes wide now
as he stared at her disbelievingly. 'I don't believe
this is happening to me!' He shook his head,
looking up towards the ceiling, his gaze returning reluctantly to Fin, heaving a shuddering sigh
as he saw she was still there. 'Most people imagine they see pink elephants; I have to see "little
people"!' His gaze turned sharply towards the
door as Ella gave a snort of laughter she tried to
control but couldn't quite manage to. 'Another
one!' he gasped his dismay, his skin seeming to
take on a green sheen now.

Fin had realised the mistaken assumption he
had made almost as soon as Ella had, and had
trouble restraining her own laughter; this man
really thought she was a hallucination brought on
as the result of too much alcohol. One of the 'lit-

tle people', indeed. She might not have explained herself very well, but really...! 'You don't understand——'

'Of course I do,' he nodded firmly. 'You're one of the "little people". Are you an elf, or a pixie, or——?'

'I *run a business* called Little People!' she snapped tautly, bright spots of colour in her cheeks, her freckles standing out against the livid colour. She might be small and delicately made, but she wasn't in the least fairy-like, and her very delicacy hid a strong-willed determination.

'Hm?' The man still looked totally befuddled by the conversation, running a hand through the length of his hair.

'Little People,' Fin repeated through gritted teeth. 'It's the name of the business I run. It's on my van outside if you would care to look,' she added exasperatedly as he still didn't look convinced by this explanation.

'It is?' He began to look hopeful that he wasn't going insane after all, although the suspicion still remained in his expression. 'Perhaps I had better Ah.' He halted in the act of getting out of the bed as he looked down and obviously realised that he didn't have any clothes on.

Fin spied a pair of denims on the bedroom floor that had obviously been discarded there some time the night before, studiously avoiding looking for any other clothing he might have thrown down so carelessly as she hurried over to pick the denims up for him. 'Here.' She held them out towards him.

He took them slowly, frowning as his suspicion deepened. 'How did you know . . . ?'

She kept her gaze determinedly turned away from Ella as she heard the other woman give a choked cough to hide her squeak of guilt. 'Logic,' Fin dismissed with a briskness that defied questioning, turning away discreetly as he pulled the denims up his long legs, standing up to fasten them before padding over to the tiny window across the room that looked out over the driveway.

God, he was tall, well over six feet, powerfully built, moving with all the feline grace of a caged tiger.

Strange she should liken him to that particular animal, Fin realised with a startled jolt; the tiger had always been the animal she considered the most beautiful!

His hair was so thick and dark now that she could see it properly, the grey among the darkness more noticeable now that it curled down on to his shoulders. His face seemed harsher in profile as he looked out of the window, those incredible-coloured eyes narrowed, his mouth a thin slash of displeasure between clenched jaws.

Some of that displeasure was due, Fin would hazard a guess, to the fact that he was now fully

aware of the fool he had made of himself minutes ago, concerning her identity, some of it was
due to the colossal hangover he probably now
realised he had—and the rest was due to a hard
cynicism that certainly hadn't materialised overnight!

One of his hands still rested on the window-sill
when he turned back into the room, challenge in
every line of his hard body, cold assessment in his
eyes as his gaze raked over her without mercy.
'Just who are you?' he repeated his initial question, this time with impatience.

Fin, still squirming from the impact of that
harsh scrutiny, felt as if he had looked at her,
from the top of her bright red curls, her heart-
shaped face with its liberal smattering of freckles, down over the slenderness of her body in the
T-shirt and denims—and found her wanting.
God, she didn't just feel as if he had, she knew
damn well that he had!

She straightened, drawing herself up to her full
five feet in height, moving forward slightly to
hold out her hand in formal greeting. 'Fin
McKenzie,' she introduced herself. 'And this is
Ella Morgan, one of my assistants.'

He made no effort to take the proffered hand,
his gaze moving sharply to Ella as she stepped
reluctantly away from the doorway. 'And what
does she *assist* you at?' he drawled disparag-

ingly, making no effort to give her his own name either.

He thought *they* were the intruders! No, he didn't; Fin immediately rejected that idea: intruders would hardly have gone to the trouble of waking him up in the way they had. He was deliberately trying to make them feel uncomfortable because of his own earlier embarrassment.

Well, Fin, for one, didn't feel in the least at a disadvantage. She knew she had a perfect right to be here, and she wanted an explanation as to why *he* was here. 'I believe we are the ones who should be asking the questions, Mr...?' She paused pointedly, but once again he chose to ignore her prompting to give his own name, meeting her gaze coolly, one brow raised in calm challenge. 'We're contracted to keep watch on the cottage whenever Gail is—— She didn't tell us you were going to be here,' Fin added stubbornly, refusing to be the one put in a position of explaining herself.

He shrugged unconcernedly, crossing his arms in front of his bared chest, a plain gold watch on the wrist of his left arm. 'That's OK; she didn't tell me about you either!'

Impasse, Fin realised frustratedly. What should she do now? As far as she was aware, the man had done nothing but get drunk, very drunk, and fall asleep in Gail's bed—without Gail. Naked. Fin mustn't forget that, *couldn't*

forget it. Even now, with the denims resting low
down on his hips to cover most of his nakedness,
the tanned hardness of his chest caused her pulse
to give a leap!

And there was still that disturbing feeling she
had that she knew this man. While he was standing up like this, his very size dominating the small
confines of the room, that feeling was all the
stronger. But she had been so young that she
couldn't remember exactly...

'I'll get in touch with Gail and have her call
you,' he added with arrogant dismissal.

You may go now, Miss Whatever-your-name-
is, Fin realised resentfully. He certainly had the
damned arrogance of—— 'I shall be telephoning
her myself, Mr...?' Once again she paused, and
this time the determination in her face brooked
no argument; she *would* at least know his name
before she agreed to leave.

'Danvers,' he came back smoothly. Too
smoothly? Had he taken those few minutes' respite to give himself time to think of another
identity for himself that would protect his anonymity...? 'Jac—Jake Danvers,' he added more
confidently.

But Fin had noted the slip, couldn't help wondering if it really was significant or if she was just
imagining things where there was nothing. But
there had been that 'Jac', and, although the name
was different, the initials were the same, J.D....

She nodded abruptly, frowning, deeply disturbed. 'We'll leave you in peace now, Mr Danvers.' She gave a strained smile. 'If you should need to contact us, we're in the book,' she offered with a politeness she was far from feeling. But if he really was a friend of Gail's . . .

'Under Little People,' he acknowledged drily, the humour evident in his voice not reaching the coldness of his eyes.

'Under Little People,' she confirmed tersely, deciding then and there that she would try to contact Gail herself as soon as she got back to the office. The sooner the puzzle over this man's identity was cleared up, the better it would be for everyone.

Not least Fin's mother . . .

CHAPTER TWO

'...Just thought I should let you know, so that there's no confusion, that my uncle will be staying at the cottage for a while,' the recorded message told Fin dismissively. 'He's pretty capable of looking after himself, so I don't think you'll need to go to the cottage again until after he's left,' Gail added hastily. 'But if you could just keep a distant eye on him...?'

Fin switched the machine off as she realised that was the end of the message. The 'confusion' had already occurred. And Fin would hazard a guess on the reason Gail had asked for a 'distant' eye to be kept on Jake Danvers—that she was well aware of the fact that he wouldn't welcome any intrusion into his privacy!

She had tried to contact the other woman, once she'd got back to the office, at the telephone number she had for her in London, but there had been no reply. Gail was an actress, had been playing in a supporting role in one of London's longest-running plays for the last nine months, and so at the moment she found it easier to stay in town during the week, and usually only managed to get down to the cottage on a Sunday overnight, hence her need for Fin to keep an eye on the cottage while she was away. Fin could only assume that the other woman was either sleeping at the moment after a late night at the theatre the night before, or else she was actually out; either way, Fin hadn't actually been able to talk to her personally yet. What she had found, when she'd decided to leave calling Gail again until later in the day and got down to listening to the rest of her overnight messages, was that one of them was from Gail herself!

It didn't bother Fin that the check on the cottage was no longer necessary at the moment; they had always had a flexible arrangement on that— no doubt when Gail was 'resting' once again she would move back to the cottage permanently anyway. But *uncle*? It wasn't exactly that Fin doubted the other woman's word, it was just— well, Gail was a tall, leggy blonde with an effervescent personality, none of which, except perhaps the height, bore any resemblance to the taciturn man Fin had encountered at the cottage earlier. The facial characteristics of the two were dissimilar too, Gail's eyes a deep, deep brown, her complexion fair, her mouth wide and smiling. But if Jake Danvers wasn't really Gail's uncle, then what was he? What, indeed . . . ?

It was really none of her business, Fin supposed ruefully; Gail was twenty-five, old enough to know exactly what she was doing. And take the consequences for it!

Nevertheless, Fin's own curiosity about Jake Danvers continued, and she went out of her way later in the morning to drive past the cottage, just to see if she might not get another glimpse of him. And reassure herself of how ridiculous her thoughts concerning his identity this morning had been, she tried to convince herself.

She could see a movement out in the garden at the front of the cottage, hesitating only fractionally before turning the van down the gravel driveway, telling herself she was only making the call to let Jake Danvers know she had heard from Gail, and knew who he was now. It was a valid enough reason, but it wasn't the true one . . .

It was him out in the garden; he was pulling up weeds from the flowerbeds, didn't acknowledge the arrival of the van, or her footsteps on the gravel as she crossed to stand beside the wall, looking over at him, by even so much as a brief break in his concentration on the back-bending work.

He looked less strained than he had this morning—less hung-over, perhaps!—that grey tinge gone from his cheeks now, and instead sweat glistened on his face and body from his exertions, his skin seeming to have gone an even deeper brown just in this short time he must have spent out in the sun today, his hair falling untidily to his shoulders.

Fin's pulse skipped a beat just from her looking at the sheer animal magnetism of him, colour burning in her cheeks as he turned suddenly and caught her watching him with avid interest.

He straightened abruptly, eyes narrowing almost accusingly, almost as if he really hadn't been aware of her presence there, his attention so intent on something else. But surely not on weeding the garden, Fin doubted sceptically.

'You again!' he rasped harshly, looking down his arrogantly long nose at her. 'Maybe you aren't really one of the "little people", but you certainly can creep around like one!' he told her disgustedly.

The name of her business had been a talking point from when she had first started out, but one of her advertising slogans at the time had been that 'she came in, did the job, and left again, without bother or hindrance to her client. Almost as if she had never been there at all'. Just the way the 'little people' were reputed to do. There had been the added factor of her name, but she had always skimmed over that particular part of it.

'I didn't try to hide the fact that I was here,' she defended a little indignantly. 'I came down the driveway in the van.' She pointed to the yellow-coloured vehicle parked a short distance away.

His mouth twisted, and he almost seemed to wince at the brightness of the colour. 'You would certainly have thought I would have noticed that!' He gave a scornful shake of his head. 'But I was deep in thought,' he dismissed impatiently. 'I didn't hear you arrive at all; you could have given me a heart attack, creeping about like that,' he accused hardly.

Surely it wasn't her fault that he hadn't heard her! And she knew what she would *like* to give him!

Oh, goodness, this second visit, meant to be a conciliatory one, was turning out to be as much of a mistake as the first one had been!

'Gail rang and left a message for me.' She deliberately kept her voice light as she tried to salvage the situation by explaining her reason for being here now at all. 'She told me that you're here on a visit,' Fin smiled.

His mouth twisted with hard mockery. 'I already knew my reason for being here!'

He certainly wasn't about to make this easy for her! 'But, as you may recall, *I* didn't,' Fin pointed out softly, determined not to allow him to force her into losing her temper. Then they would really be in trouble!

He shrugged, as if her lack of knowledge concerning his presence here really wasn't his problem, his expression scathing. 'And now you do,' he dismissed, looking at her expectantly.

And, now that she had had her say, he wanted her to leave again, his gaze told her. He really was the rudest man she had ever had the misfortune to meet!

Fin straightened, any feelings of a need to be friendly towards this man, because Gail had asked her to, and because he was a stranger to the area and she would truly have liked to make him welcome, fading rapidly at his continued rudeness. Obviously he didn't want to feel welcome, just wanted to be left alone with his rudeness. Well, that was easily arranged!

She turned to leave, but a loyalty to Gail made her hesitate slightly, to try to reach him just once more. 'If there is anything you need during your stay here——'

'I'll contact the Little People.' He acknowledged the offer with a derisive inclination of his head. 'Although I don't really see the occasion arising,' he added arrogantly.

Neither did Fin. In fact, she hoped it didn't, didn't particularly want to see this man ever again, not least because of his disturbing resemblance to that other man from the past. 'I'll leave you in peace, then,' she said in abrupt farewell.

His mouth quirked, dark brows raised over mocking eyes the colour of aquamarine. 'Now that would be a novelty!' he drawled without even attempting to hide his sarcasm.

Fin knew, without needing to look in a mirror, that her freckles would be standing out lividly against the sudden redness of her face. But at that moment she didn't care about how she looked, was fighting a battle within herself to hold on to her temper. Like a lot of red-haired people, when she lost her temper it was like Guy Fawkes Night and the Fourth of July fireworks all going off at the same time. It didn't happen very often, thank goodness, but this man was pushing her to the limits of her politeness; she had never been treated with such derision in her life before!

She drew in several deep breaths of air before even attempting to speak. 'You will find, Mr Danvers...' she spoke in carefully controlled tones, relieved to find that terrible tide of anger she had felt wash over her beginning to fade; she had never lost her temper with a client yet, even if some of them could be a little difficult. But, strictly speaking, Jake Danvers wasn't her client, he was just staying in the house of someone who was, and if the worst came to the worst she would take comfort from that knowledge before she ripped into him! '...that we are a pretty friendly crowd in this area, and——'

'And Gail assured me you also respect a person's privacy!' he cut in harshly.

Fin bit back the retort she had been about to make to the accusation, thinking, really thinking, about what he was saying to her. Discretion and quiet efficiency were attributes that were clearly promised by her service, and at the moment she was breaking one of her own rules and staying here when she clearly wasn't wanted. And that was unforgivable.

She nodded abruptly. 'That's true too,' she bit out tautly, so tense that she felt her back begin to ache. 'Enjoy your stay in the area, Mr Danvers,' she added with a formal politeness that had to be forced.

'I intend to,' he drawled condescendingly, his gaze sweeping over her with mocking pity, his stance one of pure challenge still.

Fin turned away with a sharp intake of her breath, conscious of that aqua-coloured gaze on her the whole of the time it took her to walk back to the van—and it seemed to take forever!

What an insufferable man! She didn't care who he was, he had no right to treat her or anyone else in that arrogantly dismissive way that didn't just border on being insulting but definitely *was*!

And she intended settling the matter of just *who* he was at the earliest opportunity, and had the proof one way or the other in her bedroom at home. Maybe she should have gone home earlier and done that before making this second visit to him; if what she suspected was true then she might have at least had some ammunition of her own to throw at him among all his insulting behaviour! But in a way she didn't want her suspicion confirmed, knew things would be much easier if Jake Danvers was exactly who he said he was!

In the meantime she had to meet Derek for lunch, and the last thing she wanted was to be late for that; God knew, she was going to get enough hassle from him once he knew about the committee meeting this evening!

'No, it's not on, Fin,' he reacted with predictable stubbornness when she told him about the meeting once they had eaten their sandwich lunch in the café they usually frequented for that meal. She had thought he might take the news of their broken date better on a full stomach; she had been wrong, and his handsome face flushed with his displeasure.

As Derek was tall and blond, with rugged Robert Redford-like good looks, Fin had tried, on several occasions, to convince him of how wonderful he would look up on stage himself. All to no avail. He didn't believe, as a respectable accountant, that he should make himself conspicuous in that way, certainly didn't believe his clients would have much respect for someone who made such a public exhibition of themselves. Fin's 'clients' were apparently a different matter entirely!

As her accountant, which was how the two of them had first come to meet, he knew she only earnt a comfortable living doing what she did. In fact, on more than one occasion in the past he had accused her of merely playing at working. With walking the Siamese cat on its lead as her first job directly after lunch, Fin wasn't so sure that he wasn't right.

'My mother telephoned this morning and invited us both to dinner tonight, and as we already had a date for this evening I felt confident in accepting for both of us,' Derek continued reproachfully.

Then he shouldn't have done, was Fin's first thought, not when his invitation had been to take her *out* for a meal. But she knew she owed a lot of her reaction to still feeling disgruntled from her conversation with Jake Danvers earlier, that she normally wouldn't have felt this resentment; she liked Derek's parents, had always got on well with them. But Jake Danvers's rudeness had upset her, and she had come straight from that encounter to lunch with Derek.

It was because she knew that Derek's presumption in accepting the invitation for both of them wasn't really the reason she felt so irritated that she tried to answer in a reasoning tone. 'And usually I would be pleased to go, you know that,' she placated. 'But tonight's meeting really is an emergency.'

Derek looked at her exasperatedly. 'More important even than our relationship?' he challenged sharply.

The two of them had been seeing each other fairly regularly for almost six months now, and, while she didn't feel any wild racing of her pulse, or a deep yearning to spend every minute of every day with Derek, she did enjoy his company, and the dates they had together; apart from Derek's resentment towards her interest in amateur dramatics, they actually had a lot in common, and she had to admit that the idea had crossed her mind that Derek might one day ask her to marry him. But his question now sounded to her suspiciously like a direct challenge—possibly a choice between being in the play or going out with Derek.

She frowned across the table at him. 'I didn't think they were in competition with each other,' she said with slow uncertainty—because if they were it wasn't a choice she would be able to make without a lot of thought!

'They aren't, but—— Oh, Fin!' He sighed his impatience with her. 'You throw yourself one hundred per cent into everything you become involved in——'

'I didn't think that was such a bad thing,' she frowned, having always tried to see through to the end any commitment she made—which was why she never made commitments lightly.

'It is if that one hundred per cent doesn't include me!' Derek complained irritably, his hand moving to clasp hers across the table. 'Fin, we're supposed to be a couple——'

'You're being unfair now, Derek,' she cut in dismissively. 'I don't complain about the fact that you play squash once a week, that you go to the gym three nights a week after work——'

'Because they were well-established patterns of my life when we first started going out together,' he claimed defensively. 'You surely aren't suggesting I give those up?'

Heaven forbid! 'Of course I'm not.' She shook her head with a rueful smile, gently removing her hand from within his; this was only a café, in the middle of town, in the middle of the day, not a romantic candle-lit restaurant! 'I'm just claiming the same right to have my own interests without—complaint from you. I was already involved with the Sovereign Players when we met, too,' she rushed on as she could see he was about to pick her up on her choice of words; but what else could she call it? 'Admittedly I wasn't actually acting in the last production,' she conceded. 'But I was involved.'

'But——'

'I really have to go, Derek,' she told him briskly after a brief glance at her wrist-watch. 'I have a lot to get done this afternoon.'

He eyed her resentfully as she prepared to leave. 'And dinner with my parents this evening?'

'I've just finished explaining why I can't go out with you this evening,' she said exasperatedly, not at all impressed with the scowling displeasure on his face. 'Give your parents my apologies. They'll understand,' she said with certainty as he still glared at her.

'Maybe they will,' he grated with a nod of his head. 'But *I* don't! Perhaps you need to sit down and rethink your priorities, Fin,' he suggested hardly.

She grimaced at his stubborn anger. 'I made a commitment when I went on to the committee of the society; nothing in my life has changed for me to even think about breaking that commitment.' She sighed her impatience.

Derek's expression remained implacable. 'What about your commit——? Is that what all this is about, Fin?' he asked with sudden suspicion, eyes narrowed. 'Are you trying to force some sort of declaration from me about our relationship by your stubbornness over this? Because if you are, it's——'

'I'm not!' she snapped, furious—if he could only see it!—at even the suggestion that she would even think of stooping to such subterfuge. She wasn't even sure what her answer would be if he ever should propose, let alone want to force the issue in any way! She was doing *exactly* what she claimed she was: honouring a commitment. 'I think we had better just leave this subject alone for now, Derek,' she told him tautly. 'Before one of us——' and she wasn't sure which one it was going to be! '—says something they will later regret.' She drew in a controlling breath. 'Why don't you telephone me later, and——?'

'You probably won't be at home!' He eyed her resentfully still.

It was obvious, to Fin, at least, that he wasn't in the mood to be reasoned with at all, that they were only making the situation worse by continuing to talk at all. 'Derek, maybe *you're* the one who needs to sit down quietly and rethink your priorities,' Fin said quietly.

He looked alarmed at the finality in her tone. 'What do you mean?'

'I'm not really sure.' She frowned, chewing on her bottom lip. 'Maybe——'

'Look, I'm sorry if I've been a bore, darling,' he cajoled regretfully, reaching across the table for her hand once again, smiling encouragingly. 'Maybe I have been a bit unreasonable—all right,' he nodded, his smile a little strained now, 'a lot unreasonable,' he conceded tightly. 'I'm a bad-tempered...!' He shook his head self-disgustedly. 'I know it's no excuse for my behaviour just now, but I've had one hell of a morning; please forgive me?' He attempted a little-boy look that didn't quite come off—perhaps he was right about his decision not to go on the stage! 'Of course I'll call you later, Fin,' he smiled again. 'Just put my foolishness down to disappointment at not being able to spend the evening with you after all.'

And his parents, she could have added, but didn't... God, he made it sound as if they would be forgoing a romantic evening together, when in reality it would be nothing of the sort, not under the watchful eyes of his parents! She liked the Soameses very much, found his father sweet, if a little henpecked, his mother always warm and friendly. But, as Derek was their only child, and at twenty-seven he was still a bachelor, they tended to view all his girlfriends with an eye to their being his future wife. And, although Fin knew by the warm welcome she always received from them that they approved of her, it was still a little unnerving to be constantly under inspection when in their company. Or, at least, to *feel* as if she was.

She gently squeezed Derek's hand before releasing it. 'I shouldn't be too late back tonight, if you do want to call me ... ?'

He nodded, obviously reassured by her smile. 'And if you do manage to finish early enough we could still go out for a quiet drink together.'

'Yes,' Fin agreed vaguely, not wishing to get into another argument, but already sure in her own mind that the meeting tonight would go on for some time. But there was no point in upsetting Derek again now by telling him that, and she did have an appointment to get to... 'Talk to you later,' she told him distractedly as she bent to kiss him lightly on the cheek.

Fido, the Siamese, enjoyed his walk that afternoon, as usual. His name wasn't really Fido, it was something exotically unpronounceable, which his stockbroker owner shortened affectionately to Filly. But Fin called him Fido for the simple pleasure of watching the expression on people's faces when she was out walking him on the extended lead she kept in the van for him, and she brought him back to her by calling out 'Fido', and this arrogant-looking Siamese cat appeared from whatever spot he had been exploring at the time—usually the dustbins!

Richard, the cat's owner, assured her that his little darling could only eat fresh fish lightly steamed, but Fin knew from experience that the 'little darling' would sink his delicate little white teeth into anything, given the chance—including her ankles if he was feeling particularly disdainful of the world. Which he very often was!

Maybe in future she should start to call him *Jake*...!

She had deliberately not thought of how objectionable his behaviour had been during her second visit this morning, but he really was the most arrogant, insufferable, totally obnoxious individual she had ever had the misfortune——

Her indignant thoughts were brought to an abrupt end by a loud cry that sounded like a baby in distress! And when she turned around it was to find that, during her preoccupation with Jake Danvers, Fido had wrapped his lead twice around a lamp-post and was now protesting loudly at the confinement to his movements. Another few seconds and Fin would probably have found herself flat on her backside on the pavement when the lead tightened at her end!

'Thanks for the warning,' she ruefully told Fido as she untangled him from the lamp-post, receiving an indignant nip or two from pointed white teeth for her trouble. 'I probably deserved it,' she crooned softly as she stroked the cat's silky fur, his chocolate and milky-coffee-coloured markings of championship standard. 'My mind is firmly back on the job in hand,' Fin assured him as she placed his delicate paws back on the pavement.

Obviously thinking of Jake Danvers was dangerous to her health as well as her peace of mind!

But at the same time she acknowledged that she also knew she had omitted a few of his attributes in her earlier description of him: Jake

Danvers was also the most ruggedly attractive man she had ever seen.

But he could also be something much, much more dangerous...

'Oh, Fin, thank God I managed to catch you before you went home!' Gail breathed her obvious relief.

Fin frowned at this second telephone call from the other woman in twenty-four hours. Admittedly she hadn't spoken to Gail personally the last time, but, nevertheless, Gail's message had been clear enough.

She had only called in at the office herself on her way home to close up for the evening, this call coming through before she'd had chance to switch on the answer-machine.

'Only just,' she replied derisively, looking down ruefully at the key in her hand she had ready for her departure. 'I got your message earlier, Gail.' A little late, but she had got it! 'Everything seems in order at the cottage.' She crossed her fingers at this blatant mistruth; the last thing it had seemed at Rose Cottage today was *ordered*. 'So——'

'That's just it,' the other woman cut in agitatedly. 'It isn't in order at all. Fin, I'm worried about Jake,' she added anxiously.

Oh, dear, it was going to be another one of *those* calls, Fin realised with dismay, where she had to play a guessing game, trying to discover what was actually being said to her.

She sat down wearily in her chair. It had been a long and trying day, and she was just too tired now to play any more games. And most of the reason it had been such a trying day had been because of Gail's 'uncle'!

'In what way?' she prompted evenly; from the little she had seen of Jake Danvers, he wouldn't welcome anyone's feeling 'worried' about him!

'He—he's being difficult!' Gail seemed somewhat reluctant to put the actual problem into words now that it came down to it.

Fin sighed. 'He's your friend, Gail; I'm sure you know better than most what he can be like.'

And it really was none of *her* business if Gail was having problems with him. Sorting out personal relationships, family or otherwise, was not one of the services her agency offered; there were professional agencies for things like that. It wasn't that she wasn't sympathetic to Gail's obvious concern, it was just—well, it was *Jake Danvers*!

'So do you, by the sound of it,' Gail realised with rueful humour. 'A little of Jake goes a long way, hm?' she acknowledged drily.

'Yes,' Fin agreed tersely, glancing impatiently at her wrist-watch; time was pressing on, and she had her tea to eat before getting ready to go out to the committee meeting. She also had some-

thing else to do before she did any of those
things, and *needed* to get home.

The other woman drew in a ragged breath.
'Look, the thing is, Fin—I don't know what Jake
has told you about himself——'

'Not much,' she told her pointedly.

'No. Well.' Gail sighed. 'He's a pretty private
sort of person. Is quite fanatical about it, actually, but... Look, I've tried several times to reach
him by telephone this afternoon,' this last bit
came out in a rush, 'just to make sure he's settled in OK. But each time I called the line was
dead. I contacted the operator after the last time,
a few minutes ago actually, and she said the telephone has been *unplugged* from the connection!' Gail revealed incredulously.

It seemed a rather stupid thing to do when the
cottage was as remote as it was. But, as Gail said,
Jake Danvers was a very private person, and she
was sure he had a very good reason for discon-
necting the telephone... 'Gail,' she said slowly,
'exactly *what* is it you're worried about?'

'Oh, God, I don't know,' the other woman
said exasperatedly, and Fin had a brief image of
the usually coolly capable blonde running agitated fingers through her long tresses. 'He's become so unpredictable. He had become almost a
hermit, living out in the wilds of—— Well, from
living a very solitary sort of life, he suddenly
started flitting about all over the place; I don't

know what he's doing half the time. And now he's disconnected the damned phone!' she concluded with a wail.

Fin could hear the near-desperation in the other woman's voice now. She felt sorry for her predicament, knew Gail had a performance this evening, that there was no way she could come down here herself to find out what Jake Danvers was up to. 'Have you thought of contacting the police, if you're that worried about him?' she suggested gently.

'He'd kill me!' Gail groaned with feeling.

She didn't think now was the right moment to point out that he would hardly be able to do anything if, as Gail seemed to think—otherwise, why else was she so worried?—he might have done something desperate!

'Gail, he didn't appear the suicidal type to me, if that's any help,' she reasoned gently, vividly able to recall the hard mockery in those strange-coloured eyes, and the arrogant twist to those sculptured lips. No, he didn't look the suicidal type at all to her! Besides, if he was who she thought he was then surely ten years ago would have been the time when he might just have felt desperate enough to have taken his own life. Although she obviously had no idea what might have happened in his life during the following ten years . . .

'It isn't,' Gail snapped impatiently.

'Do you want me to drive out to the cottage and check on things there for you?' Fin heard herself offering without even being aware she was about to do such a thing. But what else could she do? Gail was obviously worried out of her mind about the damned man, and over the last year the other woman had become a friend as well as a client.

But Fin already knew it was an offer she would regret, however it turned out. She already regretted it!

'Oh, would you?' Gail pounced gratefully— almost as if that weren't what she had been angling for the whole time! 'I really would be grateful.'

'You don't know how grateful,' Fin muttered.

'Oh, but I do.' The other woman had relaxed slightly, now that she knew Fin was going to help her, the smile evident in her voice. 'I'm well aware of how bloody-minded Jake can be.'

'As long as you remember you owe me one,' Fin returned ruefully at the other woman's shameless manipulation.

'Oh, I will,' Gail acknowledged lightly. 'I have to admit, this was what I had hoped for when I called you.'

'No!' Fin said in exaggerated surprise. 'Believe me, Gail, you aren't going to win any awards with the sort of acting you've just shown me!'

'Subtle as a sledge-hammer, that's me,' Gail accepted without offence, obviously just relieved that Fin was willing to be involved. 'I have to leave for the theatre in about an hour,' she added thoughtfully. 'If you could just get Jake to give me a call before then I would be grateful.'

She very much doubted that very many people 'got' Jake Danvers to do anything unless it was something he had already decided he wanted to do—and she wasn't sure, especially with the evidence of the disconnected telephone, that telephoning Gail came under that category!

'I'll pass on your message, Gail,' she said noncommittally.

'And tell him not to disconnect my telephone again!' Gail added frustratedly.

'*You* tell him not to disconnect your telephone again—if, and when, he calls you!' Fin told her decisively.

The other woman gave an amused chuckle. 'Jake seems to have made his usual charming impact on you!' she derided.

'Oh, undoubtedly!' Her sarcasm was unmistakable, even to someone with the subtlety of a sledge-hammer! 'I've no doubt I'll speak to you again soon, Gail,' she said drily before ringing off, her humour fading as soon as she had replaced the receiver. She should have just ignored the telephone when it had begun to ring, shouldn't have answered the call; now she had to go and see Jake Danvers again. And feel the sharp edge of his tongue again, no doubt. Three times in one day was just too much for anyone!

The cottage looked picturesquely beautiful as she turned from parking the van in the driveway. But there was no Jake in the garden this time, and when she knocked on the door, albeit tentatively, there was no response, and when she turned the handles on the front and back doors she found them both locked. There was no car in the driveway to tell her whether this was just because Jake was actually out rather than just not answering her knocks, and it was impossible for her to see into the high windows of the garage itself to see if his car was parked inside. Not for the first time, at that moment, she cursed her lack of height!

She was left with no other choice: she would have to use her own key to go inside the cottage and see if Jake Danvers was there and just not answering the door. After all, she had the owner's permission to find out what had happened to him—even if the man himself was likely to be furious just at the sight of her again; he had made it pretty clear the last time that if he ever saw her again it would probably be too soon!

She could feel the palpitations in her chest as she searched through her bag for her keys, finally finding them, only to drop them on to the front step in her agitation. God, it was ridiculous to feel so nervous; she had been asked to come here, wasn't an intruder, and if——

'What the hell do you think you're doing *now*?'

She had *been* in the process of putting the key in the lock, but at the first sound of that harshly angry voice she gave such a startled leap that the hand holding the keys shot up in the air and the keys flew over her shoulder, hitting Jake Danvers in the chest with a painful thump. Fin winced as she turned just in time to see the keys make contact, although the man himself seemed unmoved by the bunch of heavy metal.

All of Fin's misgivings about the advisability of coming here at all returned with a vengeance as she slowly turned to face him fully. And then wished she hadn't: he looked absolutely furious, his arms folded across the broad width of his chest now. Tall, dark, menacing, and *absolutely furious*! So much for her excuse of coming here as a favour to Gail because the other woman was so worried about him—he didn't look as if he was the one in any danger, *she* did!

'I can't believe this!' He ran an exasperated hand through the dark thickness of his hair. '"Use my cottage," Gail said,' Jake mimicked disgustedly. ' "It's very quiet there," ' he continued scornfully. ' "No one will disturb you if you don't want them to." Disturb me!' he repeated as his eyes were raised heavenwards in open disgust. 'I've been *disturbed* constantly one way or another almost since the first moment I arrived here! As for its being quiet—my God, a hotel lobby would be quieter during the busy season!'

The fact that his criticism was completely valid, and that she was the main culprit for intruding on his privacy, didn't make her feel any better.

'What are you, Fin?' He scowled at her. 'Some sort of one-woman peace and quiet shatterer? Do you go around looking for people who just want to be left alone, and then do everything in your power to make sure that they aren't? Is this one of the services of Little People: if someone expresses a need for privacy, you make sure they *don't* get it?'

His anger seemed to be increasing, not decreasing! 'Very funny,' she grimaced, still treading very warily.

'It isn't funny at all!' he rasped, glaring at her accusingly.

Did she look as if she was laughing?

'Well?' he demanded. 'What do you want this time?'

She had to bite her tongue to stop herself from making just as angry a retort. But the last thing she needed was to get into a slanging match with this man, and that was exactly what she would do if she answered him in kind. Besides—she tried to see this from his point of view—he had just walked up on her trying to enter his temporary home with a key! Obviously he had come out of the back door while she had tried to enter through the front.

'Gail rang me,' she told him flatly, deliberately keeping all emotion from her voice. 'She thought there might be—some sort of problem here.'

Jake's eyes narrowed. 'What sort of problem?'

This man, committing suicide! Now that she was face to face with the man the mere idea of that was even more ludicrous than she had thought it earlier. She should have just insisted that Gail call the police rather than coming here herself and having to take the consequences of Gail's over-protectiveness where this man was concerned. Anyone more arrogantly assured and capable of taking care of himself, thank you very much, Fin had yet to meet!

She moistened her lips, shrugging dismissively. 'Your telephone appears to have become disconnected——'

'I know,' he nodded grimly. '*I* disconnected it!'

She had already guessed that, damn it, giving him an impatient frown. 'Wasn't that rather an irresponsible thing to do, in the circumstances?'

'What circumstances?' His eyes were narrowed.

She didn't think he would appreciate the truth! 'The cottage is pretty remote, and——'

'I *know* it's remote; why the hell else do you think I came here?' he said exasperatedly. 'For God's sake, what do I have to do to be able to actually get some sleep now that I am here?' he demanded frustratedly. 'I was rudely awakened this morning by two completely unknown women who had invaded my bedroom. And now this afternoon, when I again try to catch up on some sleep, I'm woken up by the sound of someone systematically trying all the doors of the cottage and snooping around the windows, trying to——'

'I wasn't snooping!' Fin defended heatedly, her cheeks warm with indignation. 'Gail was worried about you when she realised the telephone wasn't working! She asked me——'

'What do you mean, she was worried about me?' he cut in softly—too softly, his voice having a dangerous silky quality to it now. 'Just what,' his eyes were narrowed to steely slits, 'significance did Gail seem to think there was in the telephone being disconnected, that she felt the need to contact you and get you to come over here and check things out? My God,' he grated disgustedly as he saw the answer to that question in the guilty flush to her cheeks. 'I wanted peace,' he ground out tautly, his gaze suddenly fierce. 'I wanted *privacy*. I wanted to be able to think, uninterrupted! And instead of that I find I have two women with overactive imaginations who——'

'*One* woman with an overactive imagination,' Fin corrected with firm indignation, deciding it was past time that she make it perfectly clear that as far as she was concerned he could consign himself to the devil, that in coming here now she had only been carrying out her client's—Gail's—wishes. 'I said *Gail* was worried about you, Mr Danvers,' she added pointedly. 'Obviously her concern is sadly misplaced.'

If she had hoped to shame him into realising how selfishly he was reacting then she was out of luck. 'Obviously,' he rasped harshly. 'I don't need some Little Miss Do-gooder coming here, checking up on me just because I haven't checked in and I can't be reached on the telephone!'

The ungrateful——! She hadn't really had the time to come here at all this evening, was running on a very tight schedule as it was, and now this. It was too much! 'Would you rather it had been the police who came here, ''checking up'' on you?' she challenged, meeting his gaze accusingly. 'They were Gail's only other alternative,' she explained at his disbelieving look.

His mouth tightened with displeasure. 'The little fool,' he muttered impatiently.

Fin gave him a scathing glance. 'Obviously in more ways than one.' Gail's concern for this man was obviously a complete waste of time, and certainly wasn't appreciated.

To her surprise, the anger suddenly went out of this man who, seconds ago, had been rigidly furious with it, his expression softening to something like rueful puzzlement. His next words explained why!

'It's a lot of years since I had anyone worrying over me,' he admitted gruffly.

Oh, *God. No*. She couldn't allow herself to feel sorry for the fact that no one had cared enough about this man to worry if he bothered to answer the telephone or not. She *couldn't*! Besides, it was more likely, as she had discovered now, that he didn't want people telephoning him in the first place!

'Well, if you could just telephone Gail before she leaves for the theatre to let her know everything is OK...?' she suggested stiffly before turning away.

'Fin...?'

She turned back slowly, looking at him warily. 'Yes?'

'You forgot these!' He threw her bunch of keys at her with practised aim.

Fin only just managed to catch them, shaking her head self-derisively as she realised she had been right to feel wary when he had called out to her; it would have been too much to expect that he might actually have been going to *thank* her for coming here this evening!

As she looked up into that arrogantly mocking face, and saw the humour in his eyes, she knew he had read her self-derisive thoughts, and that he was laughing at her!

She could feel that laughter following her as she walked, stiff-backed, over to the van, keeping her head firmly averted from looking at him as she reversed the van in preparation for leaving, but she could feel the heated colour in her cheeks as she couldn't help but see the mocking salute he gave her as she passed him, standing beside the garden wall, watching her every move.

Her hands were shaking, her palms damp, her cheeks hot and unattractively flushed, and all because of that infuriating man!

As far as she was concerned, in future Gail's 'uncle' could moulder away here in *complete* peace and privacy!

Her mother and David were sharing a pot of tea in the kitchen when Fin finally got home a short time later, David probably not long in from his office himself, owner of a huge stationery company that operated world-wide and kept him very busy.

David McKenzie was tall and silver-haired, fifteen years older than Fin's mother, a widower with no children of his own when he and Jenny had met. The latter was something they had tried to change during their marriage, but after almost nine years together they had accepted that it wasn't to be.

It was a great pity it had never happened for them, Fin had always felt. Her mother was one of those women who were naturally maternal, and enjoyed the fact.

And at forty-two Jenny McKenzie was still slim and very active, short and tiny like Fin herself, but with silky blonde curls she kept in a shoulder-length style, although her eyes were as deep a green as Fin's own.

'Hello, darling,' she greeted Fin warmly now, pouring out a cup of tea for her to join them. 'Hard day?' she prompted concernedly at Fin's preoccupied frown.

Fin immediately felt guilty for her distraction; she was wanting to go and look at those photographs in her bedroom, photographs her mother didn't even know she still had . . .

Her cheeks became flushed in her agitation. 'No, I——'

'She's in love,' David teased good-naturedly, grinning at her, a handsome man who had gone prematurely grey ten years ago. It was the constant worry of being her stepfather that had done it, he often teased her, knowing that she knew it wasn't true, that it was something that had happened to his father and his younger brother too. And the truth of the matter was that it made him look more handsomely distinguished than when his hair had simply been blond.

Fin had been both proud and pleased when this kind and wonderful man had come to her nine years ago and told her that not only did he want to marry her mother but that, if she would like it, he would also like to adopt her as his very own daughter. *If* she would like it! It had been the proudest day of her life when her name had become McKenzie, and this man her father.

'Trying to get rid of me?' she returned mockingly, sitting down at the breakfast-bar with her cup of tea in front of her.

'You know I am!' The affectionate way he ruffled her hair, as he stood up to go upstairs to shower and change into more casual clothing than the business suit he now wore, belied his words. 'I would offer Derek money to take you off our hands—but I'm afraid he might take it!' He whistled jauntily to himself as he left the room after blowing a kiss to his wife, quickly followed by the sound of his footsteps going up the stairs.

'He didn't mean it, you know,' her mother told her gently as Fin frowned down into her cup of tea.

She looked up, forcing a bright reassuring smile to her lips as she saw her mother's concern. 'I know he didn't,' she dismissed easily. 'I— perhaps I'm just a little tired. Too many late

nights. Too much hard work on the play.' And
she was starting to burble, over-explain herself.
This business with Jake Danvers certainly had her
rattled. 'I must say, you're looking particularly
cheerful tonight . . . ?' She tilted her head questioningly at her mother as she noticed for the first
time the slight flush to her cheeks and the glow in
her eyes. 'Did I interrupt something just now?'
she teased.

Her mother's mouth twisted with rebuke.
'David arrived only five minutes before you did!
No, it isn't that,' she shook her head, the flush
deepening in her cheeks. 'It's—I—— Oh, Fin!'
she cried excitedly. 'If I don't soon tell someone
I'm going to explode!' And she looked as if she
might be about to do that, clasping Fin's hands
tightly within hers.

Fin had never had any doubts about her
mother's happiness and contentment during the
last nine years of her marriage to David, and yet
at the same time she knew she had never seen her
mother quite this ecstatically happy before.
'What on earth is it?' She shook her head, her
laughter puzzled, her mother's excitement infec-
tious.

Her mother moved to close the kitchen door
before talking again. 'I don't want David to hear
us,' she explained softly, laughing throatily as she
saw the sobering effect this had on Fin; Jenny
and David had never had any secrets from each

other during their marriage; it was one of their cardinal rules, for reasons Fin was as much aware of as they were: Fin's own father had never believed in telling the truth when a lie was likely to achieve more. 'It's nothing like that,' her mother reassured her dismissively, her impatient tone telling Fin just how ridiculous that idea was. 'Darling, I think that at long last it might have happened!'

Fin stared at her blankly, sure she was supposed to make some appropriate response to that, but having no idea what 'it' was!

'I think I may be pregnant!' Her mother spoke the words almost as if she was afraid to even say them in case it should make them untrue.

'Mummy!' Fin's reaction was one of instantaneous joy, leaping to her feet to hug her mother. 'Oh, that's marvellous! Wonderful! When——?'

'I'm not a hundred per cent sure yet, darling.' Her mother's tension could be felt in the room. 'I may just be "going through the change" or something instead,' she grimaced. 'But Dr Ambrose thought it was worth having a test anyway. And he's promised to get back to me with the result first thing in the morning. The reason I don't even want to give David an idea it's a possibility is that it's our ninth wedding anniversary tomorrow; just think of the look on his face if I can tell him over our candle-lit dinner tomorrow night that he's going to be a father!'

Fin didn't need to think; she knew that if her mother was pregnant it would be the best anniversary present either of them would want.

'Oh, Fin, I'm almost afraid to hope!' her mother added shakily, her eyes filling with tears.

Fin's own happiness at the news was suddenly shadowed as another thought came, unbidden, to mind. The man at Rose Cottage. Jake Danvers. If that really were his name. And she didn't believe it was. She thought he was actually Jacob Dalton, a film director who had left Hollywood ten years ago and, as far as Fin was aware, not been heard of again.

A man who could, by his very presence here, completely destroy her mother's new-found happiness.

Or worse...

CHAPTER THREE

IT WAS him. There could be no doubt in Fin's mind now. The man at Rose Cottage was definitely Jacob Dalton.

The two magazines that lay open on her bed were ten years old now, the paper slightly greying, but the people in the black and white photographs were easily recognisable. Both magazines featured articles on the film currently being directed by the Golden Boy of the time, Jacob Dalton, starring Angela Ripley and Paul Halliwell. Jacob Dalton's wife, and Fin's father...

Angela Ripley, Fin knew, had been a raven-haired beauty with the deep blue eyes that everyone raved over. She looked tall and elegant in the photographs here, with the sort of curvaceous body that had made men turn and stare at her. Paul Halliwell looked tall, dark, and debonair, had been blessed, Fin knew, with more than his fair share of that smooth English charm that Hollywood had found so attractive in the eight-ies. *He* was the sort of man that women turned to stare at.

And standing between these two glittering film stars in the photograph was Jacob Dalton, Angela's husband, the director of the film. Taller than Paul Halliwell, dark hair cut severely short—which probably accounted for some of her uncertainty in recognising him earlier today!—even at the twenty-nine he must have been ten years ago, Jacob Dalton projected a hard cynicism that clearly showed he was impatient with the tedious demands for publicity for this latest film, that he would rather be anywhere else but standing in front of this camera.

And a few weeks later he had been. They all had. Angela and Paul had been dead, Jacob Dalton had been in hospital.

Angela and Paul had been killed in a fire at the Dalton home in Beverly Hills, Jacob Dalton only just managing to escape the same fate by escaping out of a window, nevertheless receiving burns to his body that had necessitated his being admitted to hospital, although those burns obviously hadn't been serious enough, Fin had clearly seen by his nakedness this morning, to leave any lasting scars.

Hollywood had deeply mourned the death of the beautiful woman, who had risen from a child-star of the sixties and seventies to one of the most popular and highest-paid actresses in the eight-ies, as only Hollywood could, seeming stunned by this terrible disaster that had taken their darling from them.

Paul Halliwell had been a fairly new bright and shining star, something of an unknown quantity still, with a wife and young daughter at home in England. And it had seemed, after the initial shock, that only Paul's wife and daughter remembered that he too had died in the fire.

Fin's mother had been devastated by her husband's death, unable to believe that her charmingly irresponsible husband was gone forever.

To Fin he had been a laughing man who showered her with gifts and laughter when he was 'working', and sank into the depths of melancholia and ignored her very existence when he was 'resting'!

She hadn't seen much of him at all for the six months before he had died, her father busy filming in Hollywood, his busy schedule not allowing him time off to get back to them in England. Fin's schooling had prevented them from going out to America to be with him too often either— in fact, her mother had refused to go again after their first visit there; she hated the artificiality of 'Tinsel Town', and the people who lived in it! And so they had continued to live their lives, for the main part, exactly as they had when her father was at home, Paul sending money home for his family, Fin going to school, her mother kept

busy with the various committees she belonged
to, along with her volunteer work in a local char-
ity shop. For them life had settled into a not un-
pleasant pattern.

All of that had been shattered by the death of
Paul Halliwell and Angela Ripley in that house
fire!

Still suffering from shock, her mother had insisted on travelling over to America alone to bring
back her husband's body for burial, leaving Fin
with the family of a schoolfriend for the few days
it would take her to sort out the formalities over
there.

She had come back alone too, completely
alone, white-faced, the shock deeper than ever.
Instead of bringing her husband home she had
buried him in the country he had adopted as his
own, among the people he had apparently come
to love too—most of them women, her mother
had discovered from the gossip that was so rife
there. Dozens of them. No woman, it seemed,
had been safe from the lethal Halliwell charm!

On her return Fin's mother had methodically
and systematically set about removing any evidence of her husband's very existence in their
lives—photographs, clothes, belongings, all of it
had been thrown out. His betrayal of them both
had been total, Jenny had told Fin dully, the last
letter he had written to her still among his things,
waiting to be posted, at the apartment he had

rented. In it he had told her how sorry he was but
that he had met someone else, someone he had
fallen in love with. That he wanted a divorce.

The 'someone else' he had met, Paul had explained, was Angela Ripley, Jacob Dalton's wife
for the last three years . . .

Fin looked down again at the magazine she still
held in her hand, magazines she had acquired at
the time and managed to hang on to during her
mother's rampage through the house to destroy
everything that would even remind them of Paul.
In this photograph Angela was laughing lovingly
up into Jacob's face even as the camera had
clicked. She certainly didn't have the look of a
woman involved in a torrid affair with the other
man photographed there. But she had been an
actress, after all—an even better one than any of
them had given her credit for . . . !

It had been obvious from the news that was
printed at the time of the fire, from the renewed
publicity over the tragedy every year on the anniversary of Angela Ripley's death—the most
recent one only two weeks ago—that the great
general public had had no idea of the affair between the two stars. Fin knew that her mother,
angered though she had been at the time by her
husband's betrayal, certainly hadn't wanted it to
become public knowledge either; her private humiliation was enough to cope with. But had

Jacob Dalton been aware of the affair between his wife and Paul Halliwell? Fin now wondered.

He had been noticeably silent, even for a man who ordinarily spurned publicity, after the tragedy, and once he was discharged from hospital, and after the very public funeral of his wife, it had been announced by the film company that Jacob Dalton was in need of a rest, that the strain of work, and now his wife's death, had been too much for him.

As far as Fin was aware, that 'rest' had lasted for the next ten years. Was still continuing, in fact...

The man at Rose Cottage *was* him, she was sure of it. Well, almost... Enough to feel deeply concerned, anyway.

She chewed on her bottom lip, wondering how long he intended staying in the area. Would her mother recognise him if she should see him? Would he recognise her mother? He wouldn't know Fin, she was sure of it, even a grown-up Fin, because Jacob Dalton had been noticeably absent on the day Fin's father had taken her around the studio. Having heard for so long what an ogre he was to work for, Fin had assumed that he probably didn't like children either! But he and her mother had met once, if only briefly, when Jenny had made the sad trip to America to collect her dead husband's belongings.

It was ten years ago, and maybe in normal circumstances Jacob Dalton wouldn't have remembered the unobtrusive wife of one of his stars, or Jenny him. But they hadn't been normal circumstances; their respective spouses had just died together in a fire that Jacob Dalton himself had only just managed to escape from, and, on top of that, the two film stars had been having an affair at the time of their deaths!

Jenny had come on a long way in the ten years that had elapsed since that time, had found a man she could love and trust, a man who made her, and her daughter, extremely happy; what had Jacob Dalton done with himself during the same amount of time? Not a lot, Fin would guess from his unkempt appearance. Except, perhaps—and she allowed him only a small benefit of the doubt!—consuming whisky in large quantities!

'Fin!' her mother called up the stairs to her. 'Darling, there's a telephone call for you.'

She had given a start of surprise at the first sound of her mother's voice, quickly closing the magazines and hiding them away in their usual place at the bottom of the wardrobe, panicked in case her mother should actually come up to her room, and relieved when she didn't hear the sound of ascending feet on the stairs.

Fin had never really been sure why she had obstinately held on to those two particular magazines, especially when she knew how upset her mother would be if she should discover them. But somehow she just couldn't throw them away. And thank God, in this case, she hadn't, for those photographs at least confirmed what Fin had suspected: the man at Rose Cottage was too much like Jacob Dalton for him to be anyone else!

She quickly went out into the hallway outside her bedroom before her mother should wonder why she hadn't responded to her call, looking down at her mother as she went down the stairs two at a time. 'Who is it?' she frowned.

'Delia!' Her mother rolled her eyes expressively. 'Something to do with wanting to know if you're going to the committee meeting tonight.'

Fin returned the knowing grimace; her mother was as familiar with Delia's over-caution as she was. 'I wouldn't dare do anything else!' Not many people would!

But as she talked soothingly to Delia over the telephone, making all the right sympathetic noises, hopefully *in* all the right places, a totally ridiculous, *unacceptable* realisation came to her: the answer to the problem of their sudden lack of a director for their play lay not three miles away, at Rose Cottage. A Hollywood—*ex*-Hollywood—film director, no less. Jacob Dalton...!

'Is that one of the elves or pixies?'

Fin stiffened instinctively at the sound of that

particular voice over the telephone the next morning, her fingers tightening around the receiver. 'Good morning, Mr Danvers,' she greeted smoothly, hoping none of her agitation was detectable.

This was the second consecutive morning that her first call of the day had totally disconcerted her; the last person, the very last person, she had expected to voluntarily hear from again was the man who called himself Jake Danvers! But she would recognise that mocking voice anywhere.

'The chief elf herself, no less,' he realised tauntingly, recognising her voice as easily, Fin able to visualise his cynically derisive expression as he did so.

She drew in a deep, controlling breath. 'This is Fin McKenzie, yes,' she confirmed abruptly. 'What can I do for you, Mr Danvers?'

'You told me to contact you if I was in need of anything,' he reminded in a low, suggestive drawl.

'Yes?' she prompted tautly, wishing he would just get on with whatever it was he wanted to say. But that would be too easy, wouldn't it? She doubted this man ever made life easy, for himself or anyone else.

'I need something,' he told her huskily, obviously enjoying himself—at her expense—immensely.

Fin wasn't feeling in the best of humours this morning. As she had known they would, she and the rest of the committee had spent the majority of the previous evening going round and round in circles. No one within the society was prepared to take up the directorship of the play, it had been established after *two hours'* discussion on that very subject, and then they had spent another hour deciding whom they could approach, without causing a political storm, outside their society.

And for the whole of the time they had been going round in those agonising circles Fin had known exactly who they could at least *ask*. Although the very idea of it was unpalatable to her, and she very much doubted he would even consider it; they were only a small local amateur society, after all, and he was a Hollywood film director—*ex*-Hollywood, she reminded herself again. As if that really made any difference—he was still Jacob Dalton!

And the last thing she had been expecting this morning was a telephone call from the man himself. For whatever reason!

She certainly wasn't in the mood to be the recipient of his rather warped sense of humour.

When she had finally got home from the meeting the previous evening it had been to be told by her mother that Derek had telephoned twice during the last half-hour, and when she had called him back it was to an expected frosty reception; at least she wasn't disappointed in that. Derek's disparaging remarks about the play had made it impossible for Fin even to discuss with him the problems they were having; an 'I told you so' was the last thing she had felt like coping with when she felt so tired and despondent. A little loving support would have been very welcome, but it hadn't been forthcoming, and consequently their call had ended with a certain amount of strain on both sides, and this morning when Fin had given her mother and David their anniversary present over breakfast and wished them a happy day she had had to act as if everything in her own world were rosy too!

Her mother, after brooding all night about the exciting secret she had, had looked, by this time, ready to burst with the news. Fin had shared in her tense excitement, hoped and prayed that the test result would be positive, and her mother could give David his gift over dinner this evening.

And now Fin had to deal with Jake Danvers as her first business call of the day! 'Yes?' Her irritation wasn't quite masked by the politeness she fought to attain.

'Is everything not running smoothly and with complete harmony in the land of the Little People this morning?' he came back mockingly.

PRIVATE LIVES   73

Fin drew in a ragged breath. 'Mr Danvers, I'm——'

'Not in the mood, hm?' he guessed tauntingly. 'Well, Fin—I can call you Fin, can't I?' he drawled softly. 'After yesterday I feel we know each other so well.'

They didn't know each other at all, and never would, but she really didn't care what he called her—as long as it wasn't *elf* or *pixie*!—just wanted him to tell her what his problem was and then get off the line; she had other work to do, and the truth of the matter was that the memory of his rudeness to her yesterday was still too raw for her to be able to deal with him calmly. That and the knowledge of exactly who he was . . . !

'Please do,' she invited impatiently.

'Did you have a late night? Is that why you——? Better not push my luck,' he dismissed wryly as he obviously sensed her increasingly frosty response. 'You had better call me Jake,' he invited distractedly. 'I actually telephoned because I need to know who I would contact to arrange to have a carpet cleaned,' he explained with a certain amount of rueful reluctance.

Because he was having to admit, for all his previous arrogant claims to the contrary, that he *did* need her, after all. The admission lightened her mood slightly. 'What carpet would that be?'

'The one in Gail's bedroom,' he muttered so softly that Fin could barely hear him.

What on earth had he done in there now?
Yesterday he had stunk the place out with
whisky, today he—— Whisky...? Could that
possibly be why it had smelt of the alcohol in
there yesterday, why the bottle had been lying
empty on the floor beside the bed? Could it be
that the bottle had actually tipped over at some
time and the liquid soaked into the carpet? It
sounded like a reasonable explanation to her.

'You spilt whisky all over it,' she guessed
wryly.

'How the hell did you——? An advantage of
being one of the Little People, I suppose,' he accepted ruefully.

Fin refused to take the bait this time over his
continued mockery of the name of her business.
In fact, she chuckled softly. 'Something like
that,' she confirmed lightly. 'As to the carpet,
normally I would have offered to come and do
something about it myself, but in the circumstances... If you look in the *Yellow Pages* under
the heading "Carpet, curtain and upholstery
cleaners" you should be able to find someone
who can help you.'

'You really know your stuff, don't you?' he
said with grudging admiration.

'It's part of my job,' she dismissed, ready to
end the conversation.

Jake had other ideas. 'Why isn't my request
being treated as "normal"?' he prompted

sharply. 'And exactly what "circumstances" do you mean?'

He had surely made his feelings clear yesterday, concerning her initial offer of help! As to the 'circumstances', he wasn't aware of it, and Fin had no intention of telling him either, but her father had been having an affair with this man's wife ten years ago! There was surely enough reason there for her to stay completely away from him. Besides, the less contact she had with him, the less opportunity there would be for her mother to meet him too. On the days when she was really busy at work her mother often stepped in to help out; it would be disastrous for all of them if her mother should happen to get called out by this man!

'You surely haven't forgotten how disparaging you were about the service offered by the Little People when we talked yesterday,' she reminded smoothly without rancour. 'And there must be any number of companies in the telephone book who could do just as efficient a job for you— possibly better if it's something they specialise in.'

'In the *Yellow Pages*, under the heading "Carpet, curtain and upholstery cleaners",' he repeated mockingly to show her he had been listening to every word she'd said to him. 'I think Gail would rather you came and did it.'

And Gail was her client, he was reminding her. And it was Gail's cottage, *Gail's* carpet. Damn him!

'I'll be there within the hour,' she told him tightly before ringing off abruptly, angry at being put in this position. She didn't *want* to go back to Rose Cottage. Didn't want to see Jake Danvers or Jacob Dalton again!

The tinkling of the bell over the door announced the entrance of someone into her office, Fin forcing a polite smile of welcome to her lips before looking up, the smile deepening with genuine warmth as she saw it was her mother. Although thank God she hadn't arrived a few minutes earlier; her mother might not have had any idea of who she was talking with on the telephone, but Fin had, and it would have made her reaction to Jake Danvers even more stilted than it had been!

She stood up to move round the desk to hug her mother. 'You didn't tell me you were coming into town.' She frowned slightly. Mother and daughter were very alike facially, even if their colouring was different, Fin's red hair a throwback, she had been told, to a great-grandmother on her mother's side.

Her mother was still filled with the restless excitement of earlier. 'I'm on my way to see Dr Ambrose,' she explained. 'He telephoned as promised this morning, just after you left actually, but he wouldn't tell me anything over the telephone; insisted I go into the surgery.'

Fin's frown deepened at this. 'Is that usual?' she voiced her concern. 'Couldn't he have just told you yes or no over the telephone?'

'Positive or negative, darling,' her mother corrected vaguely, sitting on the edge of Fin's desk. 'Knowing Dr Ambrose, he either wants to lecture me on the advisability of having a baby at my age, if it's positive!' She grimaced. 'Or else he wants to give me a shoulder to cry on if it's negative! Either way,' she shrugged, 'he wants to see me.'

Her mother was probably right, Fin realised ruefully; Dr Ambrose was one of the old-fashioned type of family doctors that were few and far between nowadays, the sort that seemed more like a family friend than the physician.

Nevertheless, Fin still felt anxious. 'You'll call me as soon as you've seen him,' she prompted, knowing that, 'either way', *she* was going to be worried too; her mother *was* a little old to be having another baby, but if it turned out she wasn't pregnant after all she was going to be very upset about it. It was a pity in a way that David didn't yet know about the pregnancy test; he would have known best how to deal with Jenny's initial disappointment if it was negative. But Fin knew she dared not risk her mother's surprise by confiding in David herself—that would be unforgivable. She would just have to keep her fingers crossed—and anything else she could think of!

'That was the reason I popped in, really.' Her mother straightened, glancing at her wrist-watch. 'I have to get along for my appointment now, but how about meeting me for lunch later? We can either celebrate or commiserate,' she grimaced, obviously not at all sure which it was going to be!

Fin certainly wasn't in the mood for another one of Derek's lectures at lunchtime about her involvement with the amateur dramatic society, and if she made the excuse that she couldn't meet him because she was having lunch with her mother he could hardly object, could he? She wouldn't even have to speak to him and so run the risk of a lecture anyway; she could leave a message with his secretary. Coward, a little voice inside her whispered mockingly. But she ignored it.

'Lovely,' she accepted her mother's invitation. 'Now I'll have to get going myself,' she realised. 'Within the hour', she had told Jake Danvers, and the minutes were ticking away fast. She hurried into the adjoining room to get out her carpet-shampooing equipment.

Her mother watched her as she checked the equipment over. 'Emergency?'

'Helpless male needing the carpet cleaned after a little accident before the lady of the house gets home,' she dismissed a little unfairly; the last thing Jake Danvers could be accused of being was 'helpless'. A lot of other things, perhaps, but certainly not helpless!

'See you later, darling.' Her mother gave her a glowing smile as they parted outside the office. Fin watched her mother walk down the street, a beautiful woman who radiated happiness and contentment with her life.

Fin couldn't help wondering how long that would continue if her mother should realise exactly whose carpet she was hurrying off to clean. God, she must never know!

'So you and your fellow elf concluded yesterday that I had drunk the whole contents of the bottle of whisky before falling into a drunken stupor,' Jake Danvers drawled drily.

Fin straightened slowly, her back aching. For the last half an hour she had been working on the carpet in Gail's bedroom to try to eliminate the overpowering smell of whisky; no wonder he had decided he had to get something done about it— if anything, it was even worse today than it had been yesterday!

'That particular joke is starting to wear a little thin, Mr Danvers,' she told him wearily, not seeming, for all her exertions, to have made the slightest impression on the smell of whisky in the carpet.

And the whole of the time she had worked Jake Danvers had sat in the bedroom chair, watching her. Very disconcerting—even if he was fully clothed today!

'Sorry,' he drawled—but he didn't look it! 'But I was right about the whisky, wasn't I?' he murmured with some amusement.

No doubt he was very often right about a lot of things, Fin thought disgruntledly, back on her hands and knees, scrubbing at the carpet. If he was always so right he should have got something done about this carpet earlier, not let it soak in and dry before calling in help!

'For your information, Fin McKenzie,' he continued mockingly, 'the night I arrived here I went to bed suffering from the effects of a little whisky—and a lot of jet lag! I had only flown in from the States that morning, and then I had to drive up here; I was exhausted by the time I finally fell into bed. Which is probably the reason I didn't notice I had knocked the *almost full* bottle of whisky over on the carpet,' he added pointedly, brows raised.

Now that she looked at him more closely he did look a lot better today, the lines of strain mostly gone from beside his eyes and mouth, slightly more relaxed in his manner too.

His hair was freshly washed and gleaming, very dark, his eyes almost luminously beautiful against his tanned skin, the firm power of his body obvious in the black jeans and black sweat-shirt he wore, the sleeves of the latter pushed up to his elbows, revealing his muscled forearms. He was much more alert today too, obviously no longer suffering from jet lag, which made him even more potentially dangerous!

'I see.' Fin's attention returned earnestly to the carpet, her tongue between her teeth as she concentrated on the task in hand, finally looking up uncertainly as she sensed he was watching her with narrowed eyes. 'What is it?' She frowned, self-consciously putting a hand up to her face; maybe she had inadvertently put a dirty mark on it, or there was a cobweb in her hair—she didn't think Gail had cleaned under this bed since the day she had first moved in two years ago!

He shrugged. 'I was expecting you at least to ask which part of America I had just flown in from!'

The less she knew about this man, or where he had been, the better! 'I was "respecting your privacy",' she reminded, brows raised pointedly.

He grinned in acknowledgement of the taunt—and it completely transformed his face! He looked almost boyish, his eyes warm, his teeth white and even against his tanned skin, two endearing dimples in his cheeks.

'*Touché*, Fin.' He gave an inclination of his head, sitting forward in the bedroom chair now, the lean strength of his hands resting on top of his

denim-clad knees. 'Is it Mrs McKenzie or Miss?'
he asked softly, his gaze suddenly intent on her
flushed face.

Fin sat back warily on her heels, eyeing him
uncertainly. Until nine years ago her name hadn't
been *McKenzie* at all, but Halliwell; although she
didn't think that was what he was asking! 'I'm
not wearing a ring,' she dismissed, holding up her
bare left hand as proof that she wasn't even en-
gaged.

Jake shook his head. 'That doesn't seem to
mean a thing any more. My own wife didn't——'
He broke off abruptly, frowning darkly, his expression suddenly savage. 'What the hell——?'
He stood up agitatedly, the relaxed mood of a few
seconds ago completely gone now as he crossed
the room to reach down to clasp Fin by the arms
and pull her effortlessly to her feet in front of
him.

Even as Fin looked up at him apprehensively
his head was lowering to hers and his mouth
ground down on her lips with fierce demand.

She was too stunned by the suddenness of it all
to do more than stand immobile within the confines of his tight embrace, his arms like steel
bands as he bent her body into the hardness of
his, every muscle and sinew outlined against her
softness.

By the time she had recovered from the shock
enough to make any show of protest at his rough

behaviour, Jake had eased the pressure of his mouth against hers, his lips now searching, exploring, the tip of his tongue probing over the edge of her teeth, all the more erotic because it only promised the deeper thrusting movement but didn't give it.

The movement of Fin's hands on to his shoulders changed from one of protest to one of acquiescence as her hands moved up into the thickness of the hair at his nape, entangling in the thick curling waves as she pulled him down to her.

Their mouths moved searchingly together now, tasting, probing, tongues licking, shivers of delight running the length of Fin's spine as Jake's hands moved restlessly up and down her back before settling possessively on her hips and pressing her into the hard throb of his body.

Fin's senses were going wild. She hadn't been expecting this from this man, for him to kiss her in this way, hadn't wanted him to—at least, she hadn't *known* she wanted him to. But she was certainly responding to him, burning sensations leaping through her body at the touch of his lips and hands, a hot, melting ache between her thighs as his body moved against hers.

But she could feel the need in Jake for more than just this, much more, and even in her own arousal she knew it was impossible, impossible because of *who he was*!

'We can't!' She pulled back protestingly, her eyes dark with passion, her lips slightly swollen from his kisses, a languid fluidity to her body that gave lie to her protest.

A lie it was impossible for him not to be fully aware of!

Jake shook his head. 'Fin, you—— What the hell ...?' He looked down at her with puzzled eyes as he pulled the book from the back pocket of her denims that had stopped him cupping her into him, his face darkening ominously as he looked down at the script for *Private Lives*.

It had become such second nature to Fin over the last month to carry the script around in her pocket, so that she could sit and study her lines during any spare moment that she had, that she didn't even know she was doing it any more, just picked it up every morning from beside her bed and put it in her pocket.

It was obvious from Jake's expression, from the way he held the script as if it might burn him, his breath sharply indrawn as he flicked through the pages and saw the part of Sibyl highlighted in pink, that he was deeply disturbed by its presence anywhere near her—or him!

He looked down at her with eyes gone suddenly icy, all hot desire wiped away in the matter of seconds it took him to recognise exactly what it was he held in his hand. 'Why do you have this?' he rasped coldly, his gaze accusing.

Fin swallowed hard, moistening lips that suddenly felt dry with the tip of her tongue. 'Our local am-dram society is putting that play on at the end of the month——'

'And you are playing the part of Sibyl,' he cut in disgustedly. 'An actress!' he accused scathingly. 'My God, a damned *actress*!' He looked at her now as if the very sight of her made him feel ill, almost throwing the script back at her.

She wasn't quick enough to catch it, fumbling as she tried to do so, watching in horror as it only narrowly missed the bucket of water she had been using to clean the carpet.

She looked back at Jake, shivering as she saw the cold rejection in eyes filled with contempt. 'Jake, will you just let me——?'

'Get out of my way!' He brushed roughly past her on the way to the bedroom door. 'And make sure you're gone before I get back!' He slammed out of the room, and then seconds later out of the cottage too, and she heard the sound of the garage door opening, and then a car engine roaring into life before being driven away at speed.

Fin stood alone in the bedroom, her arms wrapped protectively about her body as she began to shiver on this warm June morning...

CHAPTER FOUR

'POSITIVE, Fin. Positive, positive, *positive*!' Her mother almost leapt up and down on her chair when she told her the news as they sat across from each other in the restaurant.

Fin had guessed what the result of the test had been as soon as she had seen the barely suppressed excitement on her mother's face when she entered the restaurant minutes ago and saw her already seated at the table! Much as her mother had tried to suspend the moment, teasing Fin a little when they greeted each other, it had been virtually impossible for her to do so any longer, the announcement bursting out of her almost as soon as Fin had sat down.

Fin's own pleasure was tempered by a slight worry. 'And why did Dr Ambrose want to see you?' she frowned.

'Oh, it was as I told you,' her mother dismissed easily. 'I'm a little old to be pregnant again. There will be tests and things, but I expected that—it's normal procedure with older prospective mothers. Yes, I know I sound as if

I'm quoting from a textbook,' she looked a little sheepish. 'But that's probably because I am! As soon as I even suspected I might be pregnant I read all the information I could on older mothers. Dr Ambrose was quite impressed with my knowledge,' she announced with satisfaction. 'So much so that he's warned me against even *thinking* about a home delivery—he's convinced I'll try to do everything myself from now on!'

Fin moved to clasp her mother's hand now that concern was out of the way, almost as excited at the prospect of the baby as her mother was now. 'When?'

'According to the dates I was able to give him, Dr Ambrose thinks the baby should be due about——'

'Oh, I didn't mean when is the baby due,' Fin cut in teasingly. 'I wanted to know when you and David indulged in this passionate encounter that has resulted in my little brother or sister!' God, how strange that sounded. At twenty-one, probably twenty-two by the time the baby was actually born, it was going to seem a little odd to suddenly have a sibling.

Her mother chuckled softly. 'That could be a little difficult to say; there have been so many occasions——'

'I was only joking!' she interrupted hastily. She knew her mother and David did have a very loving relationship, but, like most children, no matter what age they were, she found it awkward to think of her parents making love together. Although the proof that Jenny and David did exactly that was going to be all too evident very soon, with her mother's being so naturally slender. 'David is going to be thrilled.' She felt emotionally overwhelmed for both of them, knowing by how wonderful David had always been with her, what a wonderful father he was going to make to the baby.

'Yes,' her mother agreed dreamily. 'I can hardly wait to tell him.'

By the time her mother did tell David the news Fin was well into that night's rehearsal. And without the firm guidance of a director it was a shambles, to say the least.

Delia was acting as prompt during this production as she had through most of the others the society had put on over the years; no one would even have dared to try and usurp this niche she had made for herself! But in Gerald's defection she had decided she should be the one to take over as acting director until a replacement could be found. Her autocratic manner and total insensitivity to the amateur artistic temperament had Annie Grey, the woman playing the part of Amanda, ready to throw in her script by the time Delia allowed them a break part-way through the evening!

'Bossy old cat!' Annie glared at the older woman across the village hall they rented for their rehearsals, lighting up a cigarette with agitated movements. 'Considering she doesn't even attempt to act herself, she's very eager to tell everyone else how they should do it!' she added furiously.

Delia's method of direction, mainly head-on conflict with the cast, did leave a lot to be desired, Fin admitted. But the truth of the matter was that they had all been pretty dreadful tonight, fluffing lines, if not actually forgetting them altogether.

And Fin knew that she was probably more guilty of the latter tonight than any of them; her thoughts were simply in too much turmoil for her to be able to concentrate on the play at all—so much for 'the play must go on'!

She was pleased for her mother and David, couldn't have been happier about their prospective parenthood, but at the same time she was very much aware of the complication of Jacob Dalton—— Oh, God, even thinking of him by that name could be dangerous! She could, however remote the possibility, inadvertently say it in front of her mother. *Jake Danvers* was a definite complication.

Not least because of her own reaction to him...

She had been trying so desperately all day to put the memory of the kisses they had shared from her mind; and failing miserably!

She had never responded to Derek's kisses in that way, had never responded to *any* man's kisses in that way before. She had wanted Jake Danvers to make love to her earlier, hadn't cared *who* he was at the time! But what did that make of her feelings towards Derek?

She had to stay away from Jake Danvers in future, had to hope that at this very minute he was packing his bags ready to leave. For her mother's sake she truly wished that; for herself she hoped for something completely different! Which was totally disloyal to Derek. They had been seeing each other for almost six months now, and, although she hadn't initiated Jake Danvers's kisses, at the back of her mind she still knew she should have put a stop to them much sooner than she had. If she cared for Derek at all... Which, of course, she did. Didn't she...?

When she got out of the rehearsal at only ten o'clock, Delia finally having called a halt to the rehearsal when it had become obvious that nothing was going to go right that night, Fin immediately telephoned Derek, needing the reassurance of spending time with him, hoping they could have that drink together she hadn't been able to make last night.

She hadn't seen him since yesterday lunch-time, having telephoned him this morning and explained about meeting her mother for lunch today, a fact he had accepted with good grace, considering how irritated he had been with her the evening before.

But there was no answer at his flat now, she realised disappointedly after letting the telephone ring a dozen times. It wasn't one of his usual nights for going out, but she couldn't exactly blame him for having done so; it couldn't be much fun sitting at home on his own.

But it was still only ten past ten when she got out of the telephone box, far too early for her mother and David to have returned home yet, especially now, when they had something so momentous to celebrate. And, after the awful evening she had already had, Fin didn't relish returning home to an empty house either. She should have joined the rest of the cast when they had decided to go to the local pub and drown their sorrows. But it was really too late to turn around and go back there now. Besides, she didn't think she was up to returning the banter, good-natured as it might be, about Derek's unavailability. She had tried to make light-hearted excuses for him, but Derek's disapproval of the society was felt even if he hadn't come right out and said it to their faces, and so he had done lit-tle to endear himself to its members. Not that

that particularly bothered him—in fact, he was rather pleased about it—but it could make things a little awkward for Fin. Like now!

Quite how she ended up driving down that particular lane, past that particular driveway, that particular cottage, Fin wasn't absolutely sure, but as the engine of the van suddenly began to splutter and cough like a smoker with his first cigarette of the day, she wished herself anywhere *but* down this particular lane, driving past this particular driveway, this particular cottage, the van coming to a slow stop even as she prayed that it wouldn't.

She didn't believe it, knew that the chances of this happening had to be a million to one, but after a quick look at the petrol gauge she realised she was running out of petrol!

She had meant to fill up the tank earlier today, but with everything else that had happened she had completely forgotten.

Of all places, she had to run out of petrol *here*. It was like a caricature of that old theme, 'I've run out of petrol, darling—we'll have to find somewhere to stay for the night'. Rose Cottage was the only habitation for a couple of miles, and this country lane wasn't exactly heaving with traffic either; Fin hadn't seen another vehicle since driving down it.

What was Jake Danvers going to make of her knocking on his door at ten-thirty at night, claiming she had run out of petrol?

She couldn't do it, would rather walk the two miles or so in the dark to the nearest cottage to this one than face his derision and open speculation!

Besides, Rose Cottage was in darkness, from what she could see from the road, and she certainly wasn't willing to rouse him from his bed so that she could use his telephone to call a taxi home. Of course, she had her own key to the cottage, but there was no way she could just go into it without waking the man who slept upstairs to make the telephone call; that amounted to trespassing. Besides being very embarrassing for her if Jake Danvers did happen to discover her there, it also wouldn't be very good publicity for her business if she was accused of breaking in!

No, she decided stubbornly, she would walk the couple of miles to the next cottage, and hope that the inhabitant *there* hadn't already gone to bed, too!

She took a torch from the back of the van before locking up and starting her walk, jumping nervously at any strange sound as she did so. God, she would have to stop watching those late-night horror films on the television! The trouble was, it all looked so safe on that little screen, far removed from her, but out here in the dark, with owls hooting without warning, twigs snapping under scurrying feet, dark clouds passing constantly over the huge globe of the moon, it seemed all too real!

She berated herself for her own silly stupidity as she walked the next mile, a walk that seemed twice as long in the darkness, the beam given off by the torch her only light most of the time, the moon almost constantly hidden by those clouds.

And then the arc of approaching car headlights lightened the nervousness of her thoughts; surely no one would be callous enough to just drive past a lone woman as she walked along the road, obviously in some trouble, even if the car was going in the opposite direction?

Lone woman? Suddenly Fin wondered if it would be such a good idea for the car to stop after all; one heard such strange stories nowadays of women whose cars had broken down being picked up and—— Before she could make her mind up whether she should stay put or dodge into the hedge beside the road, the sweeping arc of the car headlights as it came around the corner pinned her in the beam like a mesmerised rabbit lined up for the slaughter. Oh, God...!

As she had been sure it would, the car swept to a halt on the opposite side of the road. The model of the car was unrecognisable in the darkness, but it was long and sleek, the window opening on the driver's side with an electric whoosh, the ticking-over of the engine like a giant cat's purr.

'Lost your broomstick?' taunted an all-too-familiar voice.

A voice Fin knew she wasn't in the least surprised—in view of the location of her latest disaster!—to hear, for all that she wished it had been anyone else in this car but *him*. But it had already been one of those evenings.

She crossed over the road to stand beside the car, Jake Danvers's features looking dark and saturnine as the moon suddenly came out from behind a cloud at that moment and threw his face into stark outline.

'Elves and pixies don't have broomsticks,' she told him drily, any awkwardness over the kisses they had shared earlier that she had imagined she might feel the next time she saw him avoided by his return to mockery.

As her gaze focused better in the muted light offered by the headlamps of the car she could see his mouth quirk derisively before he answered her. 'I know,' he drawled pointedly.

It took a few seconds for his implication to sink in, and when it did she began to chuckle wryly. Although she couldn't help wondering at what point in their relationship she had become a witch ... !

'Tell me,' he shrugged curiously, 'who offers to help *you* when you need something done?'

'Anyone who happens along at the time,' Fin returned drily, knowing that the taunt was deserved under the circumstances. Although he didn't realise what those 'circumstances' were yet!

'In that case,' his teeth gleamed white in the moonlight as he grinned, 'can I offer you a lift somewhere, or are you enjoying a late-night stroll?'

Her mouth quirked at the absurdity of the latter suggestion; this was hardly a suitable place for a 'stroll' at this time of night! 'You can offer me a lift.'

'And?'

'And I'll accept,' she told him gratefully. 'My van ran out of petrol about a mile back down the road,' she explained ruefully, deciding to come clean as to how she came to be walking here at all.

'And you were alone at the time?' He shook his head in mock disgust. 'Fin McKenzie, you disappoint me!'

'Very funny!' But she chuckled in spite of herself.

'OK, get in.' He turned to the passenger-seat and began to throw the papers that covered it over on to the back seat.

Now that her gaze was accustomed to the half-light, she recognised the outline of the car as being that of the sports-style Jaguar; obviously, whatever this man had been doing with himself for the last ten years, he certainly hadn't made himself destitute. Although at the time he had walked out of Hollywood he had been its highest-paid director, and despite the high-profile lifestyle he had lived at the time he couldn't have spent all the millions he had earned in those few brief years of fame. However, that might not be true now; ten years was a long time...

'Thanks.' Fin turned to give him a grateful smile once she had climbed in beside him. 'But you don't have to drive me all the way home; the nearest telephone box will——'

'I'm driving you home, Fin,' he cut in firmly, putting the car into gear and accelerating forward. 'I may not appear much like the knight in shining armour,' he taunted self-derisively. 'But I'm certainly not dropping you off at a telephone box and leaving you there to wait for a taxi!'

So there! He certainly hadn't lost any of the autocratic manner he had been reputed to have the last ten years either.

But his arrogant determination to have his own way this time put her in a very difficult position; after driving her all the way home the least she would be expected to do was invite him in for a coffee. And that was the very last thing, given those *circumstances*, that she wanted to do! If she didn't ask him it would look rude and ungrateful, and if she did ask him—— Oh, God, make him not thirsty. Or her mother and David not back from their dinner yet. Either would do!

'You have an unusual name.' He spoke suddenly beside her in the darkness, cutting in on her chaotic thoughts.

She blinked across at him, frowning. 'Mc-Kenzie?' She moistened suddenly dry lips. Oh, God, if he should ever realise her name had once been Halliwell . . . ! She could see it all now, with sickening clarity, explaining to this man that her father had been Paul Halliwell. Even if he hadn't known of Angela's affair with the other man, just Paul's name would surely be enough to evoke unhappy memories.

Had Jake ever remarried? If he had his wife didn't appear to be with him now. But it was ridiculous to suppose that there hadn't been someone else in his life since Angela; look at the difference there had been in her own life the last ten years.

'I was talking about the Fin part.' He spoke to her as if she were a slightly backward child for not realising that.

Of course she had realised that; she had just been playing for time. 'Ah.' Her cheeks were flushed in the darkness, but of course he couldn't see that. 'It's not so unusual in Ireland,' she defended.

'You come from Irish descent?' he said interestedly, driving through the country roads with all the ease of an experienced driver.

'No,' she admitted with a grimace, at the same time realising how ridiculous she must sound. But she had no intention of explaining her unusual name!

They were nearing the town now, the powerful car having literally eaten up the miles, the lighting given off from the street-lamps meaning that they were no longer in darkness.

Jake turned to look at her briefly at that moment with mockingly raised brows.

Fin turned away from the force of that aqua gaze. 'Turn left here,' she instructed quietly. 'Then right. Now left again. It's the second house on the left,' she said with some relief as she saw that only the light left on in the hallway still glowed, evidence that her mother and David weren't home yet. No doubt the happy couple would be out late tonight, celebrating. And Fin no longer had to sit here worrying about inviting Jake in. Unless, of course, the other couple should arrive home while Jake was still drinking his coffee . . . ?

At least she didn't have to worry about photographs of her father lying about the house to give away her identity, thanks to her mother. And Fin very much doubted that Jake would recognise any of the recent photographs of her mother that there were in the house; the happy woman she was now bore little resemblance to the way she must have looked ten years ago!

'Thanks,' Jake accepted when she offered him the coffee, and Fin's heart sank; until that moment she had been half hoping he would refuse.

She was very aware of him behind her as they walked down the pathway, as she unlocked the front door with her key, and as they entered the quiet intimacy of the house. And now that they were standing in the brightly lit hallway she could see just how attractive he looked in tailored black trousers, snowy-white shirt, with a discreetly patterned tie neatly knotted at his throat, and a dark checked jacket that fitted smoothly over the width of his shoulders. And his hair, she saw with some surprise, had been trimmed. Not cut short as he used to wear it, but definitely styled into more manageable dark waves.

His changed appearance made Fin conscious of her own casual clothing and appearance, wearing a pastel pink and blue track-suit, her red curls tousled by the breeze outside, her face completely bare of make-up. Well, she had only been to a rehearsal, for goodness' sake!

'I've been in town to eat,' Jake explained his own formal appearance as he saw her gaze on him. 'There's no food at the cottage,' he grimaced.

Because Gail usually telephoned her the day before she was coming down, told her what she wanted, and they delivered the supplies to the cottage for her before she arrived!

Fin knew she should really have thought of that once she knew Jake was at the cottage, but the truth of the matter was, she didn't think very clearly at all around this man.

But she was thinking a little more clearly now, a horrendous possibility occurring to her: what if, when Jake had driven into town to eat earlier, he had chosen the same restaurant as her mother and David? God, the fact that he was in the area at all was fraught with many more dangers than she had even begun to realise!

She drew in a ragged breath. 'I could——' She broke off with a gasp as the door to the sitting-room suddenly swung open and David stepped out into the hallway, her anguished gaze moving quickly past him as she waited for her mother to join him!

CHAPTER FIVE

DAVID easily followed the direction of Fin's gaze—although not her panicked thoughts, thank God! 'Your mother has already gone up to bed. She was tired after the excitement of the evening, and I—well, I was just sitting down here ... thinking.'

In the darkness. Which explained the lack of lights on in the house to warn Fin of their return home before her. She couldn't help but feel relieved that her mother had already gone upstairs; this whole thing was starting to seem like a sick farce, with her mother and Jake barely missing seeing each other!

But she didn't need to wonder what David had been thinking about as he'd sat alone in the dark minutes ago, could see by the almost stunned look of pleasure on his face that he knew about the baby and was in awe of finally having a child of his own!

Fin moved forward to hug him. 'Congratulations!' she told him huskily, tears in her eyes as she looked at him lovingly. 'Mummy is feeling well?' she added a little anxiously.

He nodded assuredly. 'A little tired, as I said. And perhaps in a little delayed shock of her own,' he added ruefully. 'We've hoped for years, but now that it's actually happened...!' He shook his head dazedly, and it was as he did so that he became aware of the other man's presence slightly behind Fin, his eyes widening with questioning politeness as he realised he had never seen him before. 'We'll talk about this later, puss,' David dismissed, touching Fin gently on the cheek, and she realised with an affectionate choking of emotion that he was concerned that she should realise the baby made no difference to her own position in their lives. The glowing smile she gave him told him without words that she already understood that, had never doubted it for a moment. 'We don't want to bore your friend with family business,' he added with raised brows; she hadn't brought another man home during the six months she had been seeing Derek, and David obviously wondered what was going on.

'You aren't boring me in the least,' Jake told him speculatively as he stepped forward. 'Jake Danvers,' he introduced crisply, holding out his hand.

'David McKenzie,' David returned slowly, still looking puzzled, none the wiser for the introduction, although he was aware of the other man's strength as the two men shook hands.

'My stepfather,' Fin put in drily as the two men continued to eye each other curiously. They were both strong-looking men, but David, Fin knew, was possessed of a gentleness and a capacity for love, whereas Jake Danvers gave the impression that he wouldn't allow any such weakness into his life. And *that* was the main difference between the two men, Fin realised; David saw love as a strength, not a weakness. Perhaps that was the difference a good marriage made and one that had gone so badly wrong...

'And the event I mentioned a few minutes ago that Fin's mother and I have been hoping for,' David explained ruefully, 'is that, after years of trying and finally thinking it was too late, we're to have a baby of our own.' He swallowed hard, as if actually saying the words made it all more real to him. 'I still can't believe it.' He shook his head. 'I'm fifty-seven years old, and about to— genetically, at least——' he shot Fin a fond smile '—become a father for the first time! I think I need a drink,' he added shakily. 'Care to join me, Jake?' he offered.

'Well, Fin originally invited me in for coffee...but I would prefer a brandy,' the other man accepted lightly. 'To wet the baby's head, if you like.'

Fin felt as if her hold on the situation, such as it was, was fast slipping away from her; she couldn't allow these two men to actually become friends, and she could tell by the easy way they talked together as they all entered the sitting-room that they already liked the look of each other!

'Brandy, Fin?' David held the decanter poised over the third glass on the tray as he looked at her questioningly.

She certainly wasn't about to go out of the room to make the coffee she would prefer and leave the two men alone here together! And, anyway, she could probably do with the brandy more than the coffee; her nerves felt completely frazzled.

'Thank you,' she accepted tautly, sensing a narrowed aqua-coloured gaze on her for her evident agitation, deliberately not looking at Jake.

'Are you in the play too?' David asked in complete innocence of the situation as he handed the other man his glass of brandy.

Fin's hand shook slightly in the act of raising her own glass to her lips. David couldn't possibly know the time-bomb he had just introduced into the conversation!

'No,' Jake bit out tautly, adding no further explanation as he threw some of the brandy to the back of his throat, swallowing it without so much as a wince.

Fin knew she would have choked if she had drunk the fiery liquid down in that way; Jake might not be the heavy drinker of whisky she had assumed him to be at their first meeting, but he certainly wasn't teetotal either!

'The van ran out of petrol in the middle of nowhere,' she hastened to tell David, inwardly pleading with him not to ask what she had been doing this time of night 'in the middle of nowhere' in the first place. He returned her gaze blandly, obviously willing to let her tell this in her own way. For the moment. 'Jake was kind enough to stop and give me a lift home.' Even as she gave the explanation she knew she still hadn't told David how she'd come to know the other man at all! But the less she told either David or her mother about Jake, the better it would be for all of them.

'You were lucky Jake came along when he did, then,' David approved.

'Yes,' she bit out through gritted teeth, knowing she would rather it had been anywhere else but so close to Jake's temporary home that she'd had to run out of petrol, 'wasn't I?'

Aqua-green eyes glittered with suppressed laughter as Jake accurately read by her expression that she would rather it had been anyone *but* him that had come along and offered her assistance.

'How is the play going, Fin?' David prompted as they all sat down, the two men in chairs, Fin on the sofa. 'Your mother told me you're having problems; have you managed to find a new director yet?'

Fin couldn't look at Jake, and yet she knew of his sudden tension anyway, was well aware from his reaction yesterday to realising she was acting in a play that anything to do with the acting profession, amateur or otherwise, was likely to upset him intensely.

She shrugged. 'Delia filled in for this evening——'

'Oh, my God,' David grimaced, as familiar with Delia's high-handedness as Fin was; he should be—Delia had been his secretary until her retirement the previous year! And she ran the Sovereign Players with all the efficiency with which she had once run his office. 'Did everyone walk out?' he winced.

'Not quite.' Fin sighed at the almost truth of his guess. 'Annie came very close to it, though. I think that's why Delia had enough good sense to end the rehearsal when she did.'

'I'm surprised she even realised she had caused any tension,' David said teasingly. 'She has the sensitivity of a—— I'm sorry, Jake.' He gave the other man a rueful smile. 'It's very rude of us to be talking about people you don't know. At least, I presume you don't know them?'

'No,' Jake grated.

'Well, Fin is involved, as you might have gathered, with a local amateur production of *Private Lives*——'

'David, I'm sure Mr Danvers isn't interested in all that,' Fin quickly cut in on his lively explanation, still very much aware of the way Jake had blown up yesterday when he'd realised she was acting in the play.

'On the contrary,' Jake drawled with infuriating calm. 'I'm very interested. You're having trouble with your director?' He arched dark brows, almost challengingly, it seemed.

Fin eyed him warily, not quite trusting his mood. And she was absolutely positive, no matter what he might have just claimed to the contrary, that Jake Danvers or Jacob Dalton wasn't in the least interested in their provincial offering of the sophisticated *Private Lives*! 'That's right,' she confirmed flatly. 'He had to drop out for personal reasons,' she revealed reluctantly.

'You seem to get as much "artistic temperament" among the amateurs, Jake, as there is reputed to be among the professionals,' David said teasingly.

Fin felt her cheeks grow warm, knowing that Angela Ripley, this man's wife, had been reputed to be one of the least temperamental actresses in Hollywood. On the contrary, she had been everyone's darling. Including Fin's father's!

What would the great general public, who had placed the squeaky-clean actress on a pedestal from the time she had first appeared on their screens as a child-star of six, think of *that*?

Fin knew exactly what *she* thought of it. But it wasn't even possible to guess what Jake Danvers thought about anything. He had left Hollywood after Angela's death, didn't appear to have remarried in the time since, so perhaps that was indicative of the way he still thought of his dead wife.

'That isn't very fair, David,' Fin reproved only gently, knowing his mood was buoyant at the moment because of the baby, and not wanting to burst his bubble.

'You're right, it isn't,' he gave her an apologetic smile. 'Gerald is right to put his family before what should amount to a hobby, after all.'

Her mouth twisted. 'Derek thinks it's an obsession,' she said ruefully. 'He says a hobby wouldn't take up this much of my time.'

David shrugged. 'Maybe he's right. But if you really enjoy it that much...' He trailed off pointedly.

'Derek?' Jake prompted softly into the momentary lapse in conversation, having been listening to them intently.

'A friend of mine,' Fin told him firmly before David could make any reply, wondering just how much longer Jake intended staying; he had driven her home, been offered the obligatory drink, which he had accepted; shouldn't he now be as politely taking his leave?

But he gave no sign of preparing to go, his aqua-coloured gaze narrowed on her questioningly. 'Is he involved in the play too?'

'Heavens, no!' she dismissed with an incredulous laugh, sobering slightly as Jake continued to look at her with raised brows. 'It must be obvious from what we've already said that he isn't.' She shook her head ruefully.

'I see,' Jake nodded thoughtfully before putting the brandy glass down on the table beside him. 'I suppose I had better be on my way...'

At last, Fin sighed inwardly. Her mother was only feet away up the stairs; if she should wonder what was keeping David all this time and came down in search of him...!

She was genuinely grateful to Jake for giving her a lift home, but at the same time she wished he would now go!

He stood up, his size and height instantly commanding, returning David's smile with genuine warmth as the two men shook hands once again. Fin could see without the necessity for words that the two men *did* like each other, could see their obvious respect for each other, although she almost gasped aloud at David's next comment.

'Are you intending to stay in the area long, Jake? If you are, perhaps you would like to come to dinner one evening,' he suggested warmly. 'I'm sure my wife would like to meet you.'

Fin stared at the two men in mute horror; this man couldn't come here to dinner, *mustn't* meet her mother!

She swallowed hard as she became aware of Jake's narrowed gaze on her pale cheeks and over-bright green eyes, knowing he had realised her near-panic at the thought of his accepting David's invitation—and wondered at the strength of the emotion! Their own relationship had been a little stormy so far, but even so her reaction now must seem a little extreme to him. But she couldn't help that, her body taut, her palms feeling damp, her eyes wide with apprehension as she waited for his reply.

'I'm not absolutely certain what my plans are yet,' he finally answered slowly, still watching Fin intently, his mouth twisted with sardonic humour at her obvious discomfort. 'But I'll bear your invitation in mind, thank you,' he added gratefully. 'Take a rain check if I may?'

'Of course,' David confirmed smoothly. 'Any time you're free and feel like a little company, just give us a call. Or Fin,' he added with slight challenge in his voice.

She studiously avoided her stepfather's teasing gaze, concentrating on the saturnine man across the room. 'I'll walk you to the door,' she said tightly.

'How civilised of you,' Jake murmured close behind her as they went out into the hallway, leaving David alone in the sitting-room. 'Especially as you've been willing me to leave from the moment you realised your stepfather was still up!' he added tauntingly.

Fin spun around self-consciously, gasping her dismay at the accusation, relieved when she saw that David, at least, hadn't been witness to the conversation, Jake having closed the sitting-room door behind them when they had left. 'That's——'

'True!' Jake finished mockingly. 'What's the matter, Fin?' His eyes narrowed. 'Apprehensive as to what conclusions Derek will make of my having driven you home?'

'Certainly not!' Green eyes flashed her indignation at the suggestion. 'Derek knows he has no reason to mistrust me,' she claimed with more bravado than actual truth; Derek could be unnecessarily suspicious at times, and it was something about him she found very irritating.

'But he doesn't know he can trust *me*!' Jake murmured so softly that by the time Fin had been alerted to what he had actually said it was already too late to stop his arms going about her body as he pulled her up against him, his head swooping down and his lips taking possession of hers.

As she felt herself instantly respond, her arms moving up about his neck to hold him down to her, Fin knew that *she* couldn't trust herself—not around this man, at least!

He appealed to her immediate senses: taste— nectar; smell—tangy aftershave and a deliciously masculine smell that was pure Jake; and touch—oh, God, *touch*!

His thighs were hard as he held her body against the length of his, hands moving restlessly across her body and down her spine, their lips moving together in mutual need. Fin felt the warmth at her thighs as the moist tip of Jake's tongue parted her lips and penetrated her mouth, a sensual caress as he explored deeper.

There was no rejection of her this time, no fury, only dark passion in his eyes as he raised his head to look down at her.

She felt very young and vulnerable, totally exposed by the passion this man could produce in her at will. She didn't understand it, didn't want it, but she couldn't seem to stop it either, her breath catching in her throat as his lips slowly lowered to hers once again.

He drank from their moisture, sipped from her warmth, both of them knowing it was a frustrated passion. For now.

Oh, God, what was she thinking of? Fin realised in panic, wrenching her mouth away from the demanding pressure of his even as she pulled out of his arms. She couldn't see this man again, let alone let this, or more, happen between them again.

My God, she had *never* wanted a man like this before, was stunned at her own reaction to him— terrified might be a more honest description of how she felt at her wanton behaviour! If she wanted him that badly, would she be able to stay away from him?

'You're right, Fin,' Jake murmured gruffly. 'This isn't the time or the place for us to be indulging in this.' He shook his head with self-derision. 'Maybe you are a witch after all,' he murmured with a dark frown, running a hand through the dark thickness of his hair. 'Because for a few minutes there I actually forgot *where* we were, and that your stepfather could walk out here and see us at any moment!' He made the admission with harsh reluctance, as if despising his own weakness now that his head was clearing of the passionate intensity that had possessed them both seconds ago.

Fin knew she hadn't forgotten where they were, for that moment in time she simply hadn't cared! David could have walked out of the sitting-room into the hallway where they were, her mother could have come down the stairs, *the house could have fallen down around their ears*, and for that brief time in Jake's arms she wouldn't have cared.

His mouth twisted derisively. 'I can see you're as thrilled by that realisation as I am,' he rasped harshly, his eyes suddenly glacial, completely misunderstanding the reason for her look of horror. 'You didn't exactly resist, Fin,' he grated challengingly.

She stared up at him, unable to speak, to defend herself; she had no defence for what had just happened!

What about Derek? They had been seeing each other for almost six months, and yet twice now in the last two days her loyalty to the relationship had been put to the test, and both times she had failed miserably. Even if she never saw Jake again, where did that leave her relationship with Derek . . . ?

'I had better go,' Jake ground out savagely, as she still wasn't able to answer him. 'No doubt I'll see you again.'

Oh, God, she hoped not, as the front door to the house was quietly closed behind Jake as he left. Maybe if she didn't see him—— What difference would that make to the sham she had made of her relationship with Derek . . . ? This afternoon she could perhaps have put her behaviour down to stunned surprise on her part, but tonight as well was just too much. She knew she had ruined her relationship with Derek for the sake of a man she couldn't—*dared not*—see again!

She still looked slightly dazed when she wandered back into the sitting-room, lost in the torment of her thoughts.

'Impressive,' David murmured intrusively from across the room, where he still lounged in the armchair.

Fin blinked her puzzlement as she looked over at him. 'Sorry?'

His mouth twisted in teasing humour at her preoccupation. 'I said, your friend Jake is impressive,' he repeated patiently.

'He isn't my friend!' she snapped defensively. And there were plenty of words *she* could have used to describe him, and impressive certainly wasn't one of them!

David's brows rose at her vehemence over the claim. 'Well, he certainly isn't mine,' he said pointedly. 'Although I have a feeling,' he continued thoughtfully, 'that he's the sort of man who would make a very good friend, totally dependable,' he nodded. 'No matter what the situation.'

She didn't want to hear anything good about Jake Danvers at the moment, needed to remember he was actually Jacob Dalton, and that he was arrogantly impossible to deal with, in *any* situation.

She certainly couldn't allow herself to fall in love with him. Not *him* . . . !

But she couldn't seem to get away from at least talking about the man the next day, her mother, as they sat having breakfast together, deeply curious about the man who had driven Fin home the night before and come in for a drink.

'David said he was fascinating.' Her mother looked at her speculatively. 'I heard the voices down here, of course, but I thought it was just you and David talking, didn't realise we had a visitor. I would have come down if I had known.' She looked disappointed that she hadn't.

Fin thanked God that she hadn't as she drove to her office in her mother's car, needing to open the office before dealing with the problem of driving out to the van with the can of petrol. Her mother had offered to come out with her later in the morning, once Fin was organised for the day. In actual fact the two of them could have gone out straight after breakfast to collect the van, but the truth of the matter was that Fin needed this short respite away from discussing Jake. It still sent shivers down to her spine even to think how close he and her mother had come to actually meeting. She certainly didn't want to give herself time to dwell on her own behaviour with him the evening before. No, all she wanted was to get to work and forget about all of that for a few hours.

As if to torment that desire, her first call of the day was from Derek, and just the sound of his voice reminded her all too forcefully how she had returned Jake Danvers's kisses the night before.

She had barely lifted the telephone receiver, heard Derek's greeting, when she looked out of the window and saw the familiar sleek lines of Jake's Jaguar pulling up outside her office, and the lean length of Jake Danvers unfolding from its plush interior!

It was like some awful nightmare, Derek on the telephone, Jake about to enter her office!

'Fin? Fin, I said how did it go last night?' Derek repeated, with obvious impatience on the other end of the telephone line for her lack of response to his first query.

She was still staring out of the window at Jake in fascinated horror, filled with disbelief for his presence here this morning.

Dark sunglasses hid those incredible eyes from her gaze, but she could see from his tilted head that he was looking up at the sign above her window, that it would only be a matter of seconds before he looked in the actual window and saw her sitting here, watching him!

She gratefully took those few seconds' respite to take in his own appearance, the tanned arms covered in dark hair beneath the blue short-sleeved shirt that fitted across the width of his shoulders, faded denims fitting low down on his hips. His hair, cut in the shorter style, looked even more attractive today, Fin loving the way it curled endearingly about his ears and nape. Loving——! She dared not even *think* about that word in connection with this man!

'Fin, I know I've been a little intolerant of your theatrical inclinations the last few days,' Derek continued indignantly down the telephone line at her continued silence. 'But when I make an effort to show an interest you could at least show a little enthusiasm in return!'

Jake was closing and locking the car door now, his head turning as those dark glasses—and presumably the aqua-blue eyes too!—looked straight at her now as he approached the door to her office with powerfully determined strides.

'*Fin*!' Derek snapped his exasperation with the total silence that greeted his every remark. 'Oh, hell,' he muttered impatiently. 'Am I just talking to that damned machine after all——?'

'I telephoned your flat last night, Derek.' She spoke quickly, grimacing slightly as the office door opened and Jake strode into the room, one long, lean hand moving up to remove the sunglasses, Fin suddenly feeling pinned to the spot under the full force of that aqua-coloured gaze. 'There was no answer,' she told Derek lamely.

'Because I wasn't at home, obviously,' Derek answered defensively as he read criticism in her voice. 'You were out doing what you wanted to do, and so I——'

'Derek, I wasn't complaining,' she cut in hastily as she realised he had misunderstood her abrupt statement, deliberately breaking Jake's gaze to turn away and concentrate on what Derek was saying—before there were any more misunderstandings.

'You can't seriously expect me to just sit at home night after night, waiting for you to call when you can spare me a few minutes of your time!' Derek continued angrily as if she hadn't spoken.

That last accusation was completely unfair; she had always encouraged Derek to pursue his own hobbies and interests without complaint from her, which was one of the reasons she now found his criticism of her so—— But she wasn't about to argue that point with Derek when Jake was standing beside her, listening to her side of the conversation, at least! As she knew he was doing, his mouth twisted derisively, dark brows raised over mocking eyes.

'Shall we meet for lunch later, as usual?' she lightly suggested to Derek, wanting to end this particular conversation.

'Was there any doubt that we would?' Derek demanded indignantly; they always met for lunch, unless, like yesterday, Fin saw her mother instead. But that didn't usually happen two days in a row.

It was much too early in the morning for this sort of confrontation, especially in front of the audience she had! 'I have a client with me just now, Derek,' she told him decisively, also putting Jake Danvers firmly in his place—she hoped! 'Could we talk over lunch?'

'About what?' he instantly came back suspiciously.

'Derek . . . !' she voiced her exasperation, shooting Jake a slightly sick grimace at Derek's obvious persistence despite her own desire to end the conversation.

'Very well,' he snapped coldly. 'But I think you're behaving very oddly today.'

She was behaving oddly; his own mood hadn't exactly been placid and good-humoured just recently!

She replaced the receiver, taking a few seconds to gather her wits together before looking up at Jake. It hadn't been long enough! Her mouth went dry at the sight of him, her hands clenched together, and she could feel the warmth in her cheeks, knowing her freckles would stand out like beacons.

She swallowed hard, attempting to moisten her lips with a tongue that had suddenly gone dry too, meeting Jake's gaze as calmly as she could in the circumstances. 'What can I do for you, Mr Danvers?'

His mouth quirked, laughter in his eyes for her attempt at being businesslike. 'It's what I can do for you . . .' he answered her with husky suggestion.

Her eyes widened, her blush deepening to crimson. 'Mr Danvers—Jake——'

'Ah-ha!' he cut in with satisfaction at her use of his first name. 'And before you burst something with indignation over my last remark,' he continued in a drawlingly amused voice, 'I drove past the spot where your van ran out of petrol a little while ago, and I wondered if you would like a lift out to pick it up on my way back to the cottage.'

'Of course.' She kept her gaze steady with his with effort, feeling foolish for her previous assumption, determined not to make an idiot of herself like that again. 'It's very kind of you to offer, Jake, but my mother has said she'll drive out with me later.'

He shrugged. 'As I have to go back to the cottage that way anyway, it would save her the trouble. Especially in her delicate condition,' he added pointedly.

It did seem a bit ridiculous to put her mother to that trouble when Jake was going that way anyway, and she knew David was determined that her mother shouldn't overdo things, insisting on taking her up a cup of tea in bed this morning before he'd left for work. In fact, her mother had joked about the fact that maybe she should have got pregnant before!

Fin looked up at Jake now. 'If you're sure you have the time . . . ?'

'I'm sure,' he drawled mockingly for her obvious reluctance to accept his offer. 'Although I am expecting my time to be a little more filled for the next few weeks at least.' He sat on the edge of her desk, much too close for Fin's comfort. 'I called in and had a chat with your Delia Griffin earlier,' he told her softly.

She was hardly Fin's Delia! But that was the least of Fin's worries for now . . .

Jake looked down at her tauntingly. 'I'm your new director for *Private Lives*!'

CHAPTER SIX

Fin just stared at Jake, sure she couldn't have heard him correctly; he couldn't really have just said he had taken over as director of *Private Lives* . . . !

Of course he couldn't! This man was a famous Hollywood film director—even if that had been ten years ago; he wouldn't have any interest in directing an amateur production like theirs. She *must* have misheard or misunderstood what he had said.

But as she looked up at him, at the mockingly raised brows, that derisive tilt to his lips, she knew that she hadn't misheard at all.

And she also knew there could be no room for any doubt whatsoever in her mind now: with this offer he had indeed confirmed that he was Jacob Dalton!

Not that she had really thought there was any doubt in the first place, but she had hoped she might be mistaken, especially with her own growing attraction towards him. But his confidence now in his ability to direct the play, and that remarkable similarity between him and the photograph of Jacob Dalton, was just too much of a coincidence for there to be any further doubt.

He chuckled softly at her stunned reaction to his statement. 'Don't look so worried, Fin,' he grinned, gently mocking. 'I'm more than capable of doing it.'

She was sure he was. The question that bothered her was, why? Quickly followed by suspicion of those unknown motives. As far as she was aware, he had spent the last ten years avoiding anything to do with his past career, so why should he suddenly decide to change all that and help the Sovereign Players with this production? At least . . . she presumed he had been avoiding directing as a profession—for all she knew, he might have spent all of the last ten years working with one obscure repertory company after another under the guise of Jake Danvers! The only difference this time, and it was something of which Jake himself wasn't aware, was that *she* knew exactly who he was!

She stood up abruptly, unnerved by his disturbing closeness as much as the conversation. 'Why should you want to?' She watched him closely to see if she could read anything from his expression, but he was far too adept at hiding his emotions to give anything away.

'Why not?' He shrugged. 'I have nothing else to do at the moment. I've done it before, as I assured Delia. And she seemed more than satisfied with my capabilities,' he added tauntingly.

Fin ignored the taunt in that last remark, sure that when he wanted to this man knew just how to use his charm to his own advantage. And she was also sure that he would only have told Delia enough about himself for her to know he was qualified to take on the direction of the play!

She concentrated on that first remark he had made. 'Just what *are* you doing here, Jake?'

'I just told you.' He met her gaze unwaveringly. 'Nothing. Which is why I'm free now to help out your society with their little problem. But if you would rather I didn't . . . ?'

She would *rather* he disappear completely, not for her mother's sake now, but for her own . . . 'Yes,' she challenged, 'what would you do?'

His mouth twisted, eyes glinting with derision. 'Exactly what I've offered to do—direct the play!'

'That's what I thought,' Fin said drily. She hadn't believed for one moment that he would even consider her feelings when making his decision!

He gave a mocking inclination of his head. 'But your disapproval has been noted and logged, for future reference,' he drawled.

Her eyes widened indignantly. 'That's hardly fair!'

Good God, she was already under a severe disadvantage where this man was concerned—in fact, more than one! Her father had been about to take this man's wife from him before he and Angela Ripley were killed in that fire, she wanted to avoid her mother's meeting him, and possibly recognising him, at all costs, and probably worst of all was her own uncontrollable attraction towards him.

She didn't need, on top of all that, to have her reluctance to have him anywhere near her on a personal level prejudice his direction and treatment of her during rehearsals for the play!

Jake stood up with feline ease, placing the sunglasses firmly on the bridge of his nose, his eyes, those supposed windows of the soul, firmly hidden from her gaze.

'Life,' he murmured huskily, 'is very rarely fair, little one.' He reached up and cupped one side of her face with the warmth of his hand, the pad of his thumb gently caressing the softness of her lips. 'Let's hope you never really have to find that out,' he added harshly, stepping away from her sharply, his hand falling abruptly back to his side. 'Shall we go and take the petrol out to this van of yours and get this over with?' he rasped dismissively.

Fin bridled resentfully at this sudden change of mood on his part, angry with herself for reacting to the caress of his hand seconds ago as much as with him for breaking the contact so abruptly. 'I told you, my mother is perfectly happy to drive out with me later in the morning——'

'And I pointed out to you that I'm already here!' he reminded impatiently. 'Now let's go, shall we?' He stood pointedly beside the door.

Fin got wearily to her feet; what was the point of arguing with this man? What *was* the point?

But she didn't feel inclined towards indulging in conversation with him, her directions to a garage where they could pick up a can of petrol terse to say the least, absolutely speechless with the nerve of the man when he calmly informed her that he had already done that on his way to her office earlier!

He had been so sure of getting his own way that he had arrogantly gone ahead and bought the petrol without even discussing it with her!

After that Fin decided that if he was so damned capable then he could just get on with it. She sat in the Jaguar the whole time Jake went through the process of putting the petrol from the can into her empty tank, determinedly trying to ignore the play of muscles across the width of his back as he did so—and failing miserably, her senses aroused in spite of herself. He was one of the most sensually attractive men she had ever seen, the powerful languidity of his body a forceful stimulus.

Once he had completed the task he put the empty can into the back of her van before turning to Fin with a mocking smile as she finally got out of the Jaguar to join him at the side of the road. 'Just in case you should ever run out of petrol again,' he drawled derisively as he straightened.

Her cheeks became red at the taunt. 'I doubt that—it's never happened to me before!' Her life had never been this much of a muddle before either. 'Believe it or not, Jake,' she snapped, 'I managed perfectly well before you came along!'

Dark brows rose mockingly. 'Does that mean you're having some difficulty doing so now?' he challenged softly.

'Certainly not!' she snapped her resentment, realising that she could have worded her claim a little better than she had; *that* was his fault too. She snatched her keys from his hand, and then gave an inward groan as she realised how ungratefully she was behaving. Admittedly he was being deliberately provocative, but he could have no idea of the full reason his taunts were being so successful. She drew in a ragged breath. 'I appreciate your help——'

'Little liar!' He laughed softly at her obvious discomfort with having to thank him for anything. 'But you will,' he added gruffly. 'Thank me, I mean.'

Fin looked at him sharply. 'What *do* you mean?'

'Why, as a director for your play, of course,' he replied with feigned surprise, his expression one of innocent puzzlement. 'What did you think I meant?'

'Nothing!' she snapped, knowing he was enjoying playing with her now. 'I have to go,' she told him firmly before climbing into the van, studiously avoiding looking at him again.

'I'll see you tonight, Fin,' he told her softly, his mouth curving into a pleased smile as she looked at him sharply. 'At rehearsal, of course,' he added mockingly.

As if she needed any reminding of *that*, she inwardly fumed on the drive back into town. God, they would have been better off putting up with Delia. At least, *she* would. Fin didn't doubt for a moment that the play itself would benefit from Jake's experience. Damn him!

Derek looked just the same—in fact, Fin was sure he *was* just the same. Only Fin was different.

As she sat across the table from him at lunch she knew that she had changed since the last time she was with him. God, was it really only two days ago? It felt more like two years. But two days ago she had met Jake Danvers for the first time, and yesterday she had kissed him with all the passionate fervour she had never been able to share with Derek; could she now continue this relationship as if none of that had happened? She knew she couldn't. And she also knew Derek wasn't going to like it!

Maybe she should put off making any decision about the two of them until after the play—when Jake Danvers was out of her life, she knew she meant! No, she couldn't do that, she realised dully, knew that that wouldn't be fair to anyone, least of all Derek—would amount to just using him, in fact. Not that his presence in her life had been much protection against her attraction to Jake so far!

She drew in a deep breath, knowing that it wouldn't help to delay what she had to say; she was sure she wasn't going to be able to eat the sandwich she had ordered for her lunch anyway! 'Derek——'

'Before you say anything,' he smiled, 'I want to give you this!' He took a small, gaily wrapped present from his jacket pocket. 'I know I've been a bit bad-tempered lately, but——'

'Derek——'

'No, let me finish, Fin,' he gently rebuked. 'I have been bad-tempered to you,' he grimaced. 'Things are hectic—at work—and...well, no excuses,' he dismissed abruptly, holding out the parcel to her. 'I hope you will accept this small gift from me in apology, and believe me when I say things will improve from now on. I promise.' He squeezed her hand encouragingly as he pressed the gift upon her.

Oh, God . . . ! Fin looked down at the beautifully wrapped parcel with dismay. She had been on the brink of telling this man she didn't think they should see each other for a while, that out of fairness to him she felt it best if they left things between them until after the play, when if he still wanted to they could perhaps review the situation, see how they felt about each other after a few weeks' separation, had already started to say the words; how could she tell him that now when he had just given her a present—her favourite perfume, she discovered when she unwrapped it with shaking fingers!—and apologised so abjectly for being short-tempered with her lately? Maybe it was still the right thing to do, but Fin knew that she couldn't do it.

'It's lovely, Derek, thank you.' She returned his smile, a little strained perhaps, but she did return it.

'Good.' He sat back, relieved that his gift seemed to have patched things up between them. 'How about meeting tonight before rehearsal and having a quick drink together?' he suggested lightly. 'You see, Fin,' he gave a rueful grimace, 'I am trying!'

Yes, he was. He really was; lunch proved to be quite pleasant, despite her earlier nervousness, no snide remarks forthcoming from Derek about her need to go to a rehearsal tonight, no protest when she had to decline meeting him after the rehearsal too because she simply didn't know what time she was likely to be finished. Not with the new director now in charge; he could keep them there all night, for all she knew, was a completely unknown quantity. Where directing was concerned. She didn't want to think of him in any capacity. Didn't *want* to think of him at all...

Unfortunately that didn't seem as if it was going to be possible as she and Derek came out of the restaurant and she saw the man himself approaching them along the pavement with determined strides.

He hadn't spotted Fin in return yet as she came to such an abrupt halt at the sight of him that Derek walked out of the doorway straight into the back of her!

'Sorry,' Derek murmured ruefully, obviously wondering what the hold-up was as he clasped her shoulders to stop her being knocked off her feet completely rather than just off balance.

Fin turned briefly to give him a quick, reassuring smile before looking back to see that Jake was almost upon them now, still unaware that she was looking at him.

Probably because she wasn't alone in that! Jake had probably become immune, over the years, to the amount of female interest his powerful good looks attracted, seemed completely unaware of it now, his eyes narrowed, his thoughts inwards. But Fin could see there were several women turning to look at him admiringly. It seemed that the female population, from giggling teenagers to motherly pensioners, found his dark, saturnine looks fascinating. It was cold comfort to find she wasn't alone in that fascination!

'Fin, I have to——'

But she didn't hear the rest of what Derek 'had to' do, as at that precise moment Jake looked up and saw her. Recognition lightened his features, although his frown returned as he saw the proprietorial hold Derek had of her shoulders where he hadn't released her after steadying her. Aqua-coloured eyes suddenly blazed with unmistakable displeasure, Jake's mouth tightening, and the force of it was so strong that Fin barely resisted the impulse to physically shake off Derek's hands herself. And then she felt angry with herself for even thinking of doing such a thing just because Jake Danvers so obviously didn't like to see Derek touching her. Derek was her boyfriend, for goodness' sake; he had a right to touch her.

And several times in their brief acquaintance, a mocking voice inside her head reminded her, she had given Jake Danvers that same right...!

Jake came to a halt in front of her now, anger fading from his expression, to be replaced by humour as he seemed able to guess at her inner turmoil. 'Fin,' he greeted with husky warmth. 'How nice to see you again,' he added with smooth assurance.

Almost as if it wasn't only hours since they had last met! What game was he playing now? Whatever it was, she didn't want to play!

'Jake,' she greeted tersely. She didn't particularly want to introduce the two men, but knew she really had little choice in the matter, Derek even now looking at the other man with curiosity verging on hostility, his hands having slowly fallen back down to his sides from resting on her shoulders as he took in the sheer magnetism of the other man, thrusting his hands into his trouser pockets now, a sure sign that he was less than sure of this situation, Fin realised with dismay, knowing from the devilment in Jake's eyes now that she was going to get no help from him!

'And this must be Derek,' he drawled knowingly—adding absolutely nothing else to the statement!

Damn him, Fin thought frustratedly as she sensed Derek's deepening puzzlement over the other man. She was absolutely sure, in her own mind, that was exactly what Jake had hoped he would feel! *Damn* him, she thought again.

'Yes, it is,' she confirmed lightly. 'Of course, I've told you about Derek, but I'm afraid he knows absolutely nothing about you because I very rarely take my work home,' she added with sweet dismissal, more than meeting Jake's challenge—she hoped! 'Derek, this is a client of mine, Jake Danvers,' she introduced with a carelessness that made light of his significance.

Dark brows rose anyway at her method of introduction. They both of them knew Jake was many things—and Fin didn't really want to think of what he was, or what he was becoming to her!—but the one thing he surely wasn't was her client!

'Derek.' Jake thrust his hand out in what appeared to be a friendly gesture. Appeared...because, by the devilish glint in his eyes and the way Derek winced as he returned the handshake, Fin didn't think it had been *friendly* at all! 'Great girl—Fin,' he added lightly, his arm moving about her shoulders now as he gave her a brotherly hug. 'I don't know what I would do without her to come into my little cottage and——'

'I'm sure you would manage,' she told him through gritted teeth as she glared up at him, pointedly moving away from that warm encircling arm.

He looked unperturbed by the movement, hooking his thumbs into the belt loops on the faded denims he still wore from this morning. 'I doubt it,' he dismissed with certainty. 'And, contrary to what Fin said a few minutes ago, I really know very little about you, Derek,' he added blandly. 'Are you a client of Fin's too?' He quirked dark brows.

'Hardly,' Derek denied with scorn, and Fin could cheerfully have screamed at the way he played straight into the other man's hands by revealing in that one expressive word the contempt he felt for what she called work! 'I'm her accountant,' he told Jake dismissively.

'Ah,' Jake nodded, somehow managing to convey a wealth of meaning into that short acknowledgement. 'So you work for Fin,' he added with what Fin, at least, was sure was deliberate provocation.

As could be predicted, Derek flushed with resentment at such a description. 'I'm her accountant,' he repeated with stiff arrogance.

'That's what I just said; you work for Fin,' Jake accepted with feigned innocence—because he knew exactly how insulting he was being! 'Great name for a business, isn't it?' he added with an appreciative chuckle. 'Do you know, the first day I met Fin I actually thought she was a——?'

'Derek, it's almost two o'clock,' Fin hastily reminded Derek that he had told her earlier in the restaurant that he had to be back at the office by two o'clock because he had a meeting with a client at two-fifteen. She certainly didn't want Jake going into detail about their first meeting!

Derek frowned now, glancing at his plain gold wrist-watch. 'So it is,' he acknowledged distractedly. 'I had better get back,' he nodded, kissing her lightly on the lips. 'I'll see you tonight at seven o'clock,' he reminded softly. 'Danvers.' He straightened, nodding curtly to the other man, obviously not at all sure of him, even if he had seemed friendly enough.

The problem was, if Derek only knew it, that the very fact of Jake's being so friendly was telling enough!

But Derek didn't know it, although as he turned and disappeared into the crowd of people on the pavement Fin had the feeling by the stiff set of his shoulders that he was a man who knew he had somehow been insulted—he just wasn't absolutely sure how!

Fin turned on Jake with fiery green eyes the moment they were alone. 'I hope you enjoyed yourself!' she accused, glaring up at him disgustedly.

He looked completely unperturbed by the attack. 'As a matter of fact, I did!'

She had already known that! She had also known that, even if Derek hadn't been at the disadvantage of having absolutely no prior knowledge of the other man, that he would still have lost any verbal encounter he might have got into with Jake. The force of Jake's personality certainly didn't lessen with acquaintance!

And, seeing the two men together like that— Derek, tall, blond, smoothly handsome, formally clothed in one of the dark suits he favoured for work, and Jake, even taller, dark, ruggedly attractive, and casually dressed in denims and short-sleeved shirt—Fin had to admit— even though she hated doing it!—that Derek was also the one who came out wanting in any physical comparison between the two men!

Jake continued to meet her gaze, his mouth quirked with mocking humour, as if *he* was well aware of that fact too—at least, as far as Fin was concerned! 'So that was the quotable Derek,' he drawled derisively.

Fin's cheeks became flushed at the taunt. 'I didn't *say* that——'

'You didn't have to,' Jake mocked. 'Why didn't you tell him I'm the new director of *Private Lives*?' His eyes were narrowed now.

She drew in a sharp breath. 'Why didn't you?' she challenged defensively, knowing from experience of this man that he wouldn't have made the omission for her sake; he didn't seem to care how he embarrassed her. And the whole of the time the three of them had been in conversation she had been dreading the possibility of Jake's mentioning the fact that he was involved in the play too, had known instinctively that Derek wouldn't like her working night after night she was away from him with this man.

Jake shrugged. 'I couldn't run the risk, three weeks away from opening night, of the boyfriend of one of my leading actresses demanding she leave the play. And I only needed one look at the quotable Derek to——'

'Don't call him that!' she snapped.

His mouth twisted. 'OK. I only needed one look at your boyfriend to know that it was a possibility if anything else about the play should upset him, and finding out *I* was involved with it might have done that.'

She was sure it would, but the fact that Jake was right about that only made her feel more resentful. And he had very firmly put her in her place in *his* life too; now that he was involved with *Private Lives* he was only interested in the fact that she remain in the part of Sibyl!

Jake's eyes narrowed on her now. 'What did Derek mean about seeing you at seven o'clock tonight? There's a rehearsal scheduled——'

'For seven-thirty,' she finished tartly. 'At which time I will duly be present. But until then my time is my own,' she told him firmly.

For several long, tension-filled moments he continued to look down at her with narrowed eyes, and then he nodded slowly. 'As long as you understand I won't tolerate lateness from my cast,' he bit out icily. 'And now, if you'll excuse me; I have a lot to do before tonight's rehearsal.'

Fin watched in open-mouthed incredulity as he walked away with those same purposeful strides he had been taking when she had first spotted him a few minutes ago, those strides taking him into a stationery shop several yards down the street. She hadn't *asked* him to stop and talk to them, for goodness' sake, but that was what his manner had seemed to imply just now. In actual fact, the last thing, the *very* last thing, she had wanted was for Jake and Derek to meet. She hadn't thought the two men would like each other, and she certainly hadn't been disappointed!

And there was also that awful feeling in the pit of her stomach that, of the two of them, Derek had been made to look insignificant against Jake's stronger personality...

Her nervousness about tonight didn't lessen during the day, or during the brief time she met Derek, but when she arrived at the village hall at seven twenty-five for a seven-thirty start it was to find that Jake hadn't yet arrived.

Maybe he had changed his mind? Decided he didn't want to do it after all. Although that wasn't the impression she had got from him earlier today!

No, he would be here, she was sure of it. Maybe keeping people guessing was part of the way he worked.

All the rest of the cast were present, talking in groups of two or three over by the kitchen, probably discussing the expected arrival of their new director into their midst; she didn't doubt that Delia would have told them about him.

Even as she thought of the other woman, Delia spotted her across the room, made her excuses, and hastily came over to Fin.

'I hope you're going to be more agreeable about the appointment of our new director than the rest of the cast is being,' Delia muttered, shooting them a disgusted glance for their ingratitude. 'Once I had spoken to Mr Danvers this morning I managed to contact three of the other committee members—unfortunately you weren't one of them, Fin,' she put in with dismissive apology. 'And they were all agreed that anyone—that any genuine offer to help out should be given a trial run,' she hastily amended the fact that the other committee members, like her, had just been grateful for anyone to come forward and be brave enough to try to take this on! 'I was sure you would approve anyway, Fin,' she smiled confidently, 'as Mr Danvers first got to hear about our difficulties through you.'

And Jake had asked David for Delia's telephone number so that he might contact her, Fin had found out during the evening meal earlier!

And she couldn't fault Delia's actions, knew that the other woman had got a majority vote of the seven committee members, that she had done the best she could in the circumstances. And Fin had no doubt that Jake would pull them through this if anyone could. If he ever turned up, of course!

She was still reassuring Delia that her actions had been the right ones, when Jake walked into the hall at exactly seven-thirty.

The chatter in the room stopped instantly as the four other members of the cast became aware of his presence too, and turned to look at him, the two men with curiosity, the two women with open appraisal!

Lorna, the young girl of seventeen playing the part of the French maid, was positively open-mouthed, and Annie, blonde and beautiful Annie, in her late twenties, involved in a relationship with someone but not always entirely faithful to him, visibly preened in the presence of this gorgeous man.

And Fin had to admit that Jake did look...stunning, was probably the word, or the one David had used last night—impressive. Jake was dressed all in black, the loose black shirt unbuttoned at his throat and the cuffs turned back to just below his elbows, and black cords that fitted the muscular strength of his long legs, black shoes, highly polished, his dark hair brushed back from the angles of his face, that almost luminous quality to his aqua-coloured eyes even more startling against such austerity.

Delia left Fin's side to hurry over to him, her usual bossiness noticeably absent as even she fluffed and fussed over him.

Which was something he brushed off with a dismissive wave of his hand, stepping past her to stand at the very top of the room, not on the stage itself but just in front of it.

A pin could have been heard dropping in the silence of the room as he had crossed that distance with his cat-like tread. If anyone had dared to drop a pin. Which no one did.

'I'm Jake Danvers,' he announced evenly, looking around the room at them all, meeting each gaze in turn. 'I'm sure Delia has informed you by now that I'm here to direct the play. If any of you have a problem with that then speak now.'

Or forever hold your peace, was what instantly flashed through Fin's mind!

As Jake's steady gaze passed over each one of them again, challenging, lingering slightly longer on Fin than on the others, she felt—or was it just her imagination?—that he didn't expect there to be a 'problem'.

And there wasn't!

At least...not yet. Maybe later on there would be, but for the moment they all seemed happy to be under the firm control of Jake Danvers.

And as the evening progressed, that control didn't waver. Jake was hard, critical, a perfectionist when it came to having his instructions obeyed, and he altered several of the moves they had been rehearsing with Gerald for the last four weeks, proclaiming them too wooden, and expecting them to instantly remember those new moves.

Fin was the most guilty of forgetting, she knew, and Jake jumped on her—figuratively!— every time she did so.

But it was very unnerving for her, having to work with him at all, and she grew even more unnerved and agitated as Annie flirted with him outrageously throughout the evening.

She was jealous!

Unthinkable. Ridiculous. But while Fin felt herself grinding her teeth as Annie flirted with Jake every time he had occasion to speak to her Fin knew that that was exactly what she was.

'Can we expect you to make your entrance some time this evening, Sibyl?' drawled a hard voice edged with anger. 'Or would that be too much to ask?'

Colour flared in Fin's cheeks as she saw that she had been so distracted by the realisation of her jealousy of Annie that she had completely missed her cue for her entrance at the end of the first act. How could she be expected to think straight when even being in the same room as this man unnerved her?

But as she saw that everyone, not just Jake, was looking at her curiously she knew she couldn't offer that as an explanation for her lack of attention!

'Sorry,' she muttered awkwardly, taking her place behind the chair that was, for the moment, supposed to be a pair of french doors that she opened and went through on to the balcony—a balcony she should have gone out on to minutes ago and hadn't.

Jake looked at her coldly with rebuke for long timeless minutes before turning away. 'Amanda and Elyot, could you go back to: "Elyot—now with you here"?' Jake instructed harshly. 'And hopefully this time Fin will stop thinking of her boyfriend long enough to join the rest of us!'

There were several spontaneous titters of laughter from the others in the room, Annie looking almost triumphant at Jake's marked ridicule of her. And it was so obvious that he had been singling her out for his cutting remarks, right from the beginning of the evening when he had seemed to directly challenge her to protest at his right to step in as director of the play.

But she bit her tongue even now, even after that direct gibe about Derek, not quite sure what she might say to him if she once allowed herself to lose her temper. She doubted her hotheadedness then would allow his anonymity as Jake Danvers to remain intact, and that would be disastrous for everyone!

And so she calmly took her place, waited for her cue—and played the end of Act One better than she ever had before!

She knew she had, knew that the rest of the group thought so too, but the man sitting to the left below the stage remained noticeably silent— he wasn't even going to give her well-deserved encouragement for something she had done right, she realised.

The evening's rehearsal couldn't be over soon enough for her—she just wanted to get away from here and lick her wounds in private!

But it was almost eleven o'clock when it finally dragged to an end, was one of the longest rehearsals they had ever had, and nerves, and tempers—not Fin's, thankfully!—had been pushed to breaking-point several times by then, all of them escaping off to their respective homes as quickly as possible once it was over.

Except for Fin. It was her turn to lock up for the night and return the key to the caretaker's house. And Annie. Who had remained behind to talk to Jake, supposedly to question him on a particular point in Act Two. Fin left them to it, going through to the kitchen to tidy away the coffee-mugs from the evening, deliberately blocking out the murmur of their voices from the other room, although she heard the door close about five minutes later when they finally left, breathing a sigh of relief now that she could finally leave too—she had finished cleaning up the kitchen several minutes ago but hadn't wanted to go out into the main hall while Jake and Annie were still there.

She was exhausted, emotionally and physically, completely—— She came to an abrupt halt as she entered the main room and saw Jake there, slumped down in one of the hard chairs, Annie obviously being the one who had left a few minutes ago. Alone. And not with Jake, as Fin had assumed.

Jake looked up and saw her watching him. 'Well,' he sighed heavily, 'that was worse than I had thought it was going to be!'

Well, really!

CHAPTER SEVEN

THEY weren't the best actors in the world, Fin knew that, but then, they had never professed to be; they wouldn't be amateurs if they thought they were that good. But three weeks before the play was due to go on and they all knew their lines—only *occasionally* forgot to make an entrance!—so they weren't doing too badly. At least, Fin hadn't thought they were. Obviously Jake believed differently.

He looked up at her silence after his statement and saw the indignation on her flushed face, his mouth twisting wryly. 'I wasn't talking about your performances tonight. Any of them,' he added softly.

Fin frowned, looking at him more closely, realising that his face was very pale, lines of strain beside his eyes and mouth. And his hand shook slightly as he raised it to run it through the untidy length of his hair.

He stood up abruptly, thrusting those shaking hands into the pockets of the black cords as he sensed her scrutiny. 'The cast is good,' he bit out dismissively. 'You should have a more than passable production on your hands in three weeks' time. It's a bit patchy at the moment, but it will smooth out.'

High praise indeed from someone who had been such a hard taskmaster all evening. So what *was* worse than he had thought it was going to be?

Fin continued to look at him wordlessly, sure that when—and if!—he wanted to talk to her he would do so.

He shook his head, drawing in a shaky breath. 'I hope it didn't show tonight—God, I'll be mortified if it did!' he groaned his anguish. 'But, despite what I told the efficient Delia earlier today about my ability to direct the play, it's more than ten years since I did any directing!' The admission came out in an almost defensive rush.

Just over ten years, Fin realised dazedly. It was just over ten years since her father had died. And Angela. And since this man had directed anything. There had been no obscure repertory companies with him going under the name of Jake Danvers. He hadn't been near the profession he knew so well. That seemed incredible. What had he been doing with himself for the last ten years? How had he kept himself busy? Because he certainly didn't have the look of a man who had remained idle or aimless.

Jake looked across at her and saw her mysti-
fied expression, making an impatient movement. 'Shall we get out of here?' he rasped. 'Go
and get a drink somewhere?'

It was too late to get a drink in any of the
pubs—last orders would have been called some
time ago—but Fin's curiosity about this man was
well and truly aroused now, concerning those
missing ten years of his life. And for once Jake
seemed inclined to talk about himself.

'Perhaps we could find somewhere to have
coffee,' she nodded acceptance.

They left Fin's van parked outside the hall
while they went off in Jake's car to look for
somewhere that was open to serve them coffee.
But even that was impossible this time of night in
a small town like this one, they discovered as they
drove around. And Fin certainly wasn't going to
invite him back to her home; she had had one
lucky escape the evening before—it would be
pushing that luck a bit far to hope to get away
with it a second time.

'How about coming back to the cottage for
coffee?' Jake finally offered with a shrug. 'I
don't feel like going back there alone just yet
anyway.' He grimaced at the prospect.

'It's nice to know I have some uses!' Fin returned ruefully.

He shot her a sideways glance. 'I don't think you really want me to make any reply to that remark,' he said huskily.

She could feel the heat in her cheeks at the soft caress in his voice; thank goodness he couldn't see her blushes in the darkness! 'Coffee at the cottage will be fine,' she accepted tautly. 'But I had better go back and get my van first.'

He shrugged dismissively. 'I can easily bring you back into town later. After the coffee.'

And she would much rather have her own transport at Rose Cottage so that she could leave when *she* wanted to.

'I would rather get it now,' she told him with steady determination, studiously ignoring the mocking tilt to his lips as he easily guessed the reason for her stubbornness. 'I don't think I should leave the van parked outside the hall when there is obviously no longer anyone there, especially after the van was left abandoned on the road last night too,' she added defensively. 'The police might tow it away this time! Besides,' she said brightly, 'I have to go and put the key through the letter-box of the house of the caretaker of the hall. It's the usual practice,' she excused as he looked puzzled. 'I'll only be a few minutes behind you,' she assured, not wanting him to lose the reason as to why she was having coffee with him in the first place; she desperately

wanted to have that talk his conversation had
seemed to promise earlier.

Jake shrugged, too weary to argue the point
any longer as he ran a hand over his eyes. 'It will
give me time to make the coffee.'

And it would give Fin time to regain some of
the composure she had lost during the last few
minutes! The last thing she had been expecting
from him, after the fiasco of the evening, was
veiled flirtation, despite the fact that he had already kissed her yesterday. But then, it hadn't
really been flirting, more like mockery.

The cottage was a blaze of lights when she
turned the van down the driveway fifteen minutes later after dropping off the keys along the
way, and she remembered what Jake had said
about not wanting to go back to the cottage alone
just yet. Strange; he didn't seem the type of man
who would want to avoid his own company,
seemed pretty self-sufficient in that way. But
perhaps it wasn't his company he wanted to avoid
tonight either, but the memories that directing the
play tonight must have evoked . . . ?

He did seem preoccupied as he let her into the
cottage, holding a jar of instant coffee in one
hand; so much for 'making' the coffee—hot water, a dash of milk, and he had it! How silly of
her to have thought he might go to the trouble of
making the percolated kind, which she pre-
ferred, for her!

He absently shifted some newspapers off one
of the chairs in the tiny sitting-room, with its
chintz-covered furniture and curtains. 'Gail will
be down on Sunday.' He looked about him
slowly, grimacing at the untidiness that had en-
sued in only the few days he had been here. 'I
think I had better try and tidy up before then.' He
looked across at Fin as she sat in the chair, sur-
veying the disorder with rueful eyes. 'I don't
suppose you ... ?'

She eyed him mockingly now. 'I don't work
Sundays.' Even poor Fido had to forgo his walk
on a Sunday!

'Tomorrow would do,' Jake informed her
hopefully. 'I promise to keep it tidy then until
Gail arrives.'

Fin quirked taunting brows. 'What happened
to all that fierce independence I had from you the
other day?' she reminded pointedly.

He met her gaze blandly. 'As I recall, what I
said on that occasion was that I didn't foresee a
time when I would need your assistance,' he
drawled with perfect clarity. 'Now I do,' he
shrugged. 'I hadn't realised what an untidy slob
I've become after living on my own for years.' He
looked about the untidiness of the room with almost surprised eyes. 'I'm sure it didn't look anything like this when I arrived!' There were
newspapers lying on the chairs, and cups and
plates, the latter looking as if they might have had

a sandwich or a piece of toast on them, on the small tables dotted about the room.

Fin knew, better than most, that it hadn't been like this when he had arrived; Gail always left everything neat and tidy when she went back up to town. And, at the moment, everywhere looked decidedly untidy. Not that she could see upstairs—not that she *wanted* to tonight, either!—but it had looked just as untidy when she was up there cleaning the carpet yesterday. How could one lone man make this much mess?

'It only needs things tidying away,' she dismissed; as far as she could see, everything looked clean enough.

'Then you will come over tomorrow and help me out?' Jake pounced gratefully. 'I do appreciate it—it will certainly save Gail reading me the Riot Act! She got her temper from her father's side of the family,' he added with a grimace.

Implying that his sister, who Fin presumed had to be Gail's mother, didn't have a temper. After the way Jake had flared up at Fin yesterday she knew the same couldn't be said for Gail's *uncle*! But his words finally eliminated any doubt she might still have had concerning his relationship to Gail.

And she certainly hadn't been offering to come here to tidy up for him tomorrow when she'd made that comment a minute ago, but as Jake went back to the kitchen to make the coffee she could see that the matter was settled as far as he was concerned!

'Here we are.' He soon returned with the mugs of coffee, handing one to Fin before sitting down in the chair opposite hers. He sipped the steaming brew appreciatively before speaking again. '*Did* my nervousness show tonight at rehearsal?'

Fin frowned at how this seemed to be bothering him. 'Not so that anyone would notice!' she said drily, the memory of the razor-edge of his tongue still very much with her.

His mouth twisted wryly. 'I haven't lost my touch in the discipline area, I see,' he drawled derisively.

'You said it's ten years since you last did any directing...?' she prompted as casually as she could in the circumstances, longing to know what had happened to him during the intervening time.

'Just over,' he nodded grimly, all humour gone from his face now. 'I—used to work on a more—professional level,' he continued, if still somewhat evasively. 'But I became—sickened by the artificiality of it all, and I don't just mean the filming. I—was married then,' he added harshly, a nerve pulsing in his cheek. 'My wife died,' he stated coldly. 'And so, as I had no one else to think of but myself, I walked out on it all. I sold up, bought myself a farm and some land in England, and took up sheep farming,' he revealed ruefully.

Sheep farming? Jacob Dalton had spent the last ten years of his life farming sheep for a living? It sounded incredible!

But Fin didn't doubt that he was telling her the truth, knew that he had no reason to lie to her. But it was all the things he hadn't said, things that Fin knew anyway, that struck her so forcibly. This man had been the highest-paid director in Hollywood ten years ago, had been at the very height of his profession, had looked set to continue being so. And his wife hadn't just died, she had been Angela Ripley, Hollywood legend in her own lifetime, and she had been killed in a fire at their home that had also killed her lover, the man she had intended leaving Jacob for.

Had Jake ever known that? Had he known of the affair between his wife and her latest leading man—with Fin's father? Was that one of the reasons Jake had been so 'sickened' by Hollywood? God, there was still so much she wanted to know—and she couldn't ask this man to tell her, because to do so would reveal her own identity!

But *sheep farming*, for a man who had been as brilliant a director as this one had; she still found it hard to believe.

It took tremendous effort of will on her part to keep her expression only mildly curious. 'Did you like it?'

Jake's mouth quirked. 'Very much, as it happened. I didn't expect to,' he admitted ruefully at her raised brows. 'I bought the farm originally as a way of getting completely away from the rat race of film making, intended putting in a manager and just vegetating myself. I didn't want to think, didn't want to do anything. After two months of doing that I was climbing the walls for something to do! That's when Andrew, my farm manager, started taking me out and about with him, showing me how everything worked.' His mouth twisted ruefully. 'If I ever fall on hard times I could always apply for the job of farm manager now and know that I'm worthy of that title!' The last was said without conceit, just a complete confidence in his own capabilities.

And Fin didn't doubt it was true, was sure that whatever this man decided to do he would do it well—even as the drunken reprobate she had first thought him, he had been totally convincing!

'Why have you left the farm now?' She frowned her puzzlement. 'Bedfordshire, much as I love it, is hardly the place you would choose for a holiday when you've obviously been living in a rural area yourself for the last ten years.'

His mouth tightened. 'I needed time to think, away from everything and anyone who knows me. Gail offered me the use of this cottage, and so . . .' He shrugged.

'And so you came here, got set upon by Little People, and ended up directing the local amateur production!'

'Hm.' He gave a rueful smile at this condensed version of what had happened since his arrival here, sobering suddenly, looking across at Fin with narrowed eyes. 'Do you think you can ever go back, Fin?' he rasped harshly. 'Do you?'

She looked at him sharply. Go back to what? Was he talking about the farm? Had he tired of it after all these years and didn't want to go back to it after this short break? Or was he talking about something else completely...? My God, he wasn't talking about——

Jake stood up abruptly, pacing the small confines of the room like a caged tiger. 'I've written a screenplay.' He didn't even seem to be talking to her any more, his thoughts inward, on his inner conflict. 'I tried to stay away from the damned business and everything to do with it, but I think, after all, it must be in my blood,' he said self-disgustedly. 'The thing almost seemed to write itself,' he groaned.

But there was more; Fin could see there was much more!

'I don't even know why I did it,' he moaned, 'but I sent the damned thing to a film company, and now they want to make it.'

She had known there was more. And she could see he still hadn't finished ...

His eyes were pained. 'They wanted to talk to me about it, so I agreed to go over to the States; that's why I've only just got back from there.' He shook his head. 'They had a condition for making the film,' he revealed heavily. 'They want me to go over there and direct the damned thing myself!'

Fin knew that she gasped at this revelation, but she couldn't help herself.

Jacob Dalton, returning to Hollywood...

My God, just think what the media would make of something like that; newspapers would pay thousands of pounds now for an exclusive like this one, especially with the tenth anniversary of Angela Ripley's death so recently in their minds. Not that Fin would even think about giving them that information, not for any price, but it did help to explain what Jake was doing here under an assumed name.

Maybe the reason he had got involved in directing the play for the Sovereign Players, after a break of so many years, suddenly became clear too...

'I've been away from it all for over ten years now, Fin,' he burst out suddenly, his whole body taut with tension. '*Ten years*! God, ten days is a long time in that tinsel town!'

He seemed to have forgotten for the moment that she only knew him as Jake Danvers, that she must be wondering exactly who Jake Danvers was that a Hollywood film company should want him so badly to direct his own film. Fin didn't wonder at all, of course, but Jake couldn't realise that!

And she readily agreed with him about the memories of the people in Hollywood; her own father's death had been forgotten in a matter of the days he had just mentioned.

Jake shook his head. 'There isn't really anything to think about at all, is there?' he answered himself heavily. 'I can't do it.' He sat down abruptly.

Fin took the time to moisten her lips before speaking. 'Is it a good screenplay?' she asked, not knowing, for the moment, what else to say.

His head shot back defensively, his eyes blazing with colour. 'Of course it's a good screenplay. It's damned good!'

His complete arrogance might have been amusing in any other circumstances, but the last thing she dared do at the moment was smile! 'Then doesn't it deserve a "damned good" director too?' she said softly. 'I'm only speaking as an amateur actress, of course,' she added quietly. 'But you must be a very good film director for the film company to want you so badly.'

Jake absorbed her words, frowning darkly as he thought about them, although he was obviously deeply disturbed at the prospect of 'going back', as he had put it earlier.

'What will you do with your farm while you're away?' Fin prompted softly at his continued silence.

'I've already offered to sell it to Andrew,' he dismissed vaguely. 'It's the perfect investment for him and his new wife.' He shrugged.

Then Jake had already, without even being aware that he had done so, made his decision, had already set about severing the ties he had made in his new life in preparation for returning to his old one. But he didn't seem to have realised that that was what he *had* done, not yet, needed a little more time to be able to see that clearly...

She drew in a steadying breath. 'Then to answer your question of earlier,' she smiled, 'I don't think you can ever ''go back''; you can only ever go forward. If that going forward involves you retracing old footsteps, it doesn't mean the outcome will be the same as the first time around. The circumstances are always different, Jake,' she told him gently. '*You're* different. You aren't the same person you were ten years ago.'

'Hell, I hope to God I'm not!' he rasped bitterly.

'I'm sure you aren't,' Fin said firmly. 'None of us is. And, because you aren't either, going back won't be the same as it was before.'

He stared at her wordlessly for several long, tension-filled minutes, and as he looked at her the tension slowly left his body. 'When did you get to be so wise, Fin McKenzie?' he finally murmured softly.

She smiled wryly, putting down her empty coffee-mug, knowing instinctively that the moment of intimacy was over, that Jake now needed time on his own to really think about what had been said. 'It's probably the "little person" in me,' she said self-derisively. 'Just do me a favour,' she grinned down at him as she stood up.

He looked at her curiously. 'If I can,' he nodded slowly.

'Just don't desert us for Hollywood until after we've put the play on!'

He didn't return her smile. 'Talking of the play,' he looked at her with narrowed eyes now, 'I didn't mention it to you in front of the others earlier this evening, but I think you should know I don't allow members of my cast to drink before a performance—or a rehearsal!'

Fin returned his gaze in dumbfounded amazement. What did he——? She had met Derek in the local pub for a lager and lime at seven o'clock tonight before going on to the rehearsal. Half a pint of lager and lime could hardly be classed as 'drinking'!

And it was more than a little ungrateful of Jake to reprimand her over it all when she had just spent over an hour of her time listening to him while he poured out his troubled thoughts to her!

He stood up abruptly. 'I shall be mentioning it to the others,' he rasped. 'But I wanted to have a word with you about it privately first.'

How generous of him. How kind. How bloody damned patronising!

It wasn't until she had driven halfway home, her departure from Jake made very frostily indeed, that it occurred to her to wonder *how* Jake had even known she was in the pub if he hadn't been in there himself . . . !

CHAPTER EIGHT

JAKE was thankfully absent when Fin arrived at the cottage to clean the next day, and she hurried through the task, hoping she didn't have to see him today; if she did she might not be as speechless concerning the remarks he had made about her going to the pub before last night's rehearsal—she wasn't struck dumb through being flabbergasted by his cheek today as she had been last night!

He was right about *all* of the cottage being an untidy mess—it was. But it was easily tidied up, and the smell of whisky in the bedroom seemed to have gone for the main part now. Which was just as well, with Gail coming down tomorrow!

Was Gail really his niece? From the remarks he had made last night, Fin had thought so, but, now that she was back here at the cottage on her own, she couldn't stop the wild imaginings that went through her mind. If Gail *weren't* Jake's niece, would she be sharing the double bed in the master bedroom with him tomorrow night...?

Fin turned away from even looking at the double bed, as its very existence took on mocking implications. She had always made it a point never to question or judge her clients, deeming it none of her business what they did in their private lives. As it was none of her business whether or not Gail was really Jake's niece...

She might not be supposed to have these sort of thoughts, but that didn't stop them tormenting her anyway!

Gail was an attractive blonde, involved in the same profession as Jake himself, and so the two of them would have a lot in common—amateur dramatics surely didn't count as that!—and Fin knew that Gail thought nothing of indulging in a physical relationship with a man she was attracted to, whereas Fin—— She broke off these tortuous thoughts once again; she might be attracted to Jake, but she was *going out* with Derek! That had to count for more than a fleeting, dangerously impetuous attraction towards a man who was likely to have left here in a matter of weeks to return to the glittering world of films he should obviously never have left in the first place.

To her dismay, Jake was just climbing out of the Jaguar when she went out on to the driveway to get in the van and leave. Colour brightened her cheeks as she saw him so soon after her so disturbing thoughts minutes ago.

He straightened, holding a large carton of strawberries in one hand. 'You aren't leaving already?' He frowned as he realised that that was exactly what she had been about to do.

'I've been here over an hour,' she defended. 'Plenty of time to have tidied up, I can assure you.'

Jake strolled towards her, his masculinity a tangible thing in snug-fitting denims and a loose black short-sleeved shirt. He seemed to wear the austere colour rather a lot, but maybe it was indicative of his mood the majority of the time! Although he looked cheerful enough today. Dangerously so...

'I was expressing disappointment if that was the case, Fin, not criticism,' he told her softly, his gaze searching on her flushed face as he stood only inches away from her now, looking down at her.

She swallowed hard, inwardly chivvying herself not to be fooled by the seductive persuasion in his voice. This man's moods were mercurial, completely unfathomable; one moment he was confiding his innermost torments to her, and the next he was berating her for... He was just impossible for her to understand!

'Sorry,' she muttered. 'But I really have finished tidying the cottage, and now I have to go——'

'Why?' Jake cut in softly.

She looked at him sharply. He certainly looked more relaxed today, almost as if a great weight had been lifted from his shoulders. Maybe he had come to a decision about directing the film? Which meant he would be leaving here soon, very soon . . .

'I have to go home and learn my lines,' she told him abruptly. 'My director is very strict about the cast knowing their lines,' she added pointedly; he had snapped at all of them the night before about not being fast enough with their dialogue.

His mouth twisted at the taunt, his brows raised. 'As I recall, you always carry your script about with you.'

Her resolve tightened as she remembered his savage reaction to his initial realisation that she was in the play at all. 'Not any more,' she bit out tautly.

Jake shook his head. 'You know your lines.'

'My moves, then——'

'They're fine too,' he put in firmly.

Her eyes widened. 'But last night——'

'Fin,' he began softly, 'last night was last night. And today is today,' he added huskily. 'Last night I was your director. Today I'm your——' he paused, eyes deeply aqua '—friend,' he finished gruffly. 'Never confuse the two,' he advised lightly.

Fin frowned her puzzlement. 'Are you saying you don't?' That would certainly go part-way to explaining his differing changes of mood!

'Not any more!' he rasped harshly, all teasing gone from his deeply etched face. 'I allowed a personal relationship to interfere with my professional integrity once before, and I swore I would never let it happen again.' He looked grim at the memory.

His marriage could surely be called a little more than a 'personal relationship', Fin mused dazedly, for that must be the time he was talking about?

She remembered reading in one of the magazine articles she had at home that the film they had been making was the first time the husband and wife had worked together, and what a tragedy it had been that the film was never completed with their involvement; in true Hollywood tradition, the film *had* gone on to be made again, with a new director and male and female stars. It had been a big hit with the box-office, if not the critics, evidence that the general public took a macabre delight in imagining how the original stars would have looked. The re-filmed version had even been on television several times during the last few years, but Fin had never been able to bring herself to watch it. She couldn't help wondering if Jake ever had . . .

'Look,' Jake continued on a lighter note, holding up the punnet he held in his hand, 'I bought us some strawberries. And there's some ice-cream in the fridge, too,' he added temptingly.

'Bought "us" some strawberries?' She sounded sceptical about the probability of this claim, wondering if this was just another of those occasions when he didn't feel like being alone. Although she had to admit that he seemed more than cheerful enough, and it was rather a big punnet of strawberries for just one person, so perhaps...

He shrugged dismissively. 'I knew you were coming here today,' he reminded. 'And everyone likes strawberries and ice-cream. Don't they?' he enticed.

Fin had to admit that she was more than fond of the deliciously sweet-tasting fruit. But even so...

'You, young lady,' Jake tapped her lightly on the tip of her nose, 'will have to learn to take constructive criticism—and that's all last night was—without taking offence if you're to survive in the world of acting, even amateur, at all,' he chided lightly. 'Now let's go into the cottage and you can help me to wash these strawberries.' He strode off purposefully in the direction of the cottage without even waiting to see if she followed him.

Because he was used to giving instructions and having them obeyed, Fin realised frustratedly as she stared after him.

But her reluctance to share the strawberries with him had nothing to do with his criticism of her acting during his role as director of the play; she just didn't believe the comment he had made about her being in the pub before the rehearsal came under that heading, had felt it was much more personal than that, no matter what he might think to the contrary. Good God, she could just as easily have had a couple of glasses of wine with her evening meal at home before going to the rehearsal, and Jake would have known nothing about that! No, he had been being petty, she was sure of it, and she wasn't comfortable with that.

Nevertheless, the strawberries and ice-cream beckoned through the open door of the cottage. And something else . . . Something she just dared not think about too deeply.

'Do you like your sugar on them once they have been washed, or do you prefer to dip them?' Jake asked without looking up as she entered the kitchen and he stood at the sink washing the strawberries under the running tap-water, putting the washed ones on a piece of paper towel to dry.

'After the washing, if I'm to have ice-cream with them,' Fin accepted, moving to get the bowls out of the cupboard and the ice-cream out of the freezer; after all, she had been checking on the cottage for months, so she knew where everything was.

It seemed just as natural, ten minutes later, to find herself sitting outside on the garden lounger that lay beside Jake's, both of them indulging in a large bowl of strawberries and ice-cream!

Butterflies fluttered around them, bees buzzed from flower to flower, birds sang in the trees, and all of this beneath a gloriously clear blue sky. Almost like paradise. Except she wasn't Eve—and Jake certainly wasn't her Adam!

'There's nothing quite like a beautiful English summer's day,' Jake murmured softly, seeming to read her thoughts—or, at least, some of them!

He spoke wistfully, almost as if he was already preparing himself to say goodbye to the beauty of a lush green English summer to move to the humid heat of Los Angeles.

He would be returning to the world he rightly belonged to. It would be better for everyone when he did!

Fin put her bowl down abruptly, even though there were still some strawberries and ice-cream left, the latter melting rapidly in the heat of the day. 'I have to go,' she told Jake curtly.

He raised dark brows at her bowl. 'But you haven't finished eating yet,' he pointed out mildly.

Fin knew she couldn't eat any more now, that to do so would probably choke her. She had just realised something so disastrous, so catastrophic, that she could hardly breathe. She had fallen in love with Jake **Danvers!**

Except that he wasn't Jake Danvers, was he? He was Jacob Dalton, a man who, by his mere presence here, could shatter her mother's happiness like glass.

Fin stared at him with wide green eyes, her freckles livid against the paleness of her cheeks. Madness. Utter, and complete, madness. And yet she knew that was exactly what had happened, that she had fallen in love with this man, so that the mere thought of his leaving here, and her never being able to see him again, filled her with a cavernous despair. She was such a contradiction of emotions inside, not wanting Jake to leave for her own sake, and yet knowing he had to for her mother's.

'I can't eat any more,' she told him truthfully, swallowing hard, swinging her legs down on to the ground, her legs long and tanned beneath white shorts matched with a white T-shirt. 'I have to go,' she added abruptly as she stood up. 'I—I have to go and walk Fido.' She thankfully latched on to this legitimate excuse to leave; Richard would be wondering what had happened to her today.

Jake frowned up at her as he still lay there. 'Mind if I finish off your strawberries?' He picked up her bowl and began to eat the red fruit when she made no reply. 'Can't someone else walk the dog while you relax for a few hours?' He frowned.

Her mouth twisted wryly at the perfectly natural assumption he had made. 'Fido is a cat. Don't ask,' she warned derisively as his brows were raised incredulously.

'I don't think I'd better,' Jake grimaced. 'I suppose it was only to be expected, with you being one of the "little people", that you would have a cat with a name like Fido!'

'He isn't my cat!' she protested laughingly. 'I walk him for a friend. A client really,' she frowned. 'Who has since become a friend.'

'I suppose she would have to have done really,' Jake taunted. 'With a cat called Fido, who needs to be taken for a walk, you would need all the friends you could get!'

Her tension of a few minutes ago was fading completely as this nonsensical conversation continued. It was almost as if—— She frowned. 'The owner is a he. And——'

'Derek?' Jake questioned sharply, getting to his feet too, his relaxed teasing having disappeared now as he looked almost predatory.

'No—not Derek,' she dismissed instantly, slightly dazed at his sudden change of mood. Yet again! 'Richard is exactly what I said he was, a friend. I—believe his interest lies in a completely different direction,' she dismissed.

'Good.' Jake nodded his satisfaction with that idea, steadily holding her gaze as he moved to stand in front of her.

Fin looked up at him apprehensively, fearful in case he should touch her after her so recent realisation of her feelings for him, still astonished at the enormity of the emotion she felt towards him. Love . . . She *loved* this man!

She couldn't move, couldn't speak, as his head began a slow descent towards hers, her breath catching raggedly in her throat as his face was only fractions of an inch away from hers, his tongue flicking out moistly over her lips, sending rivulets of sensation down her spine, her lips tingling from the caress as he raised his head slightly.

Aqua-coloured eyes met hers with open desire. 'Ice-cream,' he excused gruffly. 'On your lips. I couldn't resist.'

But he made no such excuse as his lips now moved to claim hers, his arms going firmly about the slenderness of her body, hands caressing her in restless need.

Their hunger was for something much more fundamental than strawberries and ice-cream now as their mouths fused together, desire flaring up and out of control, devouring, possessing, *demanding* fulfilment.

Jake's hair felt soft and silky beneath her questing fingers as she pulled him down to her, her feet barely touching the grass now as Jake held her into the hardness of his body, raw energy claiming her in powerful demand, Fin clinging to his shoulders now, fiery passion turning her legs to jelly.

Her breasts were bare beneath the loose white T-shirt, the nipples hard and turgid as Jake pushed the material up out of his way and exposed her naked flesh to the moistness of his questing mouth and tongue, the hot lapping caress sending a warm rush of desire through her body to her thighs, an ache that made her groan with need.

Jake lay her gently down on the green grass before joining her there, his eyes dark with passion as he looked down on her loveliness, the naked beauty of her breasts, his gaze heatedly holding hers as his lips once again claimed the sensitivity of one hard, thrusting nipple, his tongue a rasping caress.

It was the most erotic experience Fin had ever known, watching Jake watching *her* as she instinctively reacted to the moist caress!

Her cheeks were flushed, her breathing shallow, every part of her body feeling as if it were on fire. She wanted to cry out, to scream and shout, tell Jake of her deepest needs.

But he already knew them, his lips trailing a path of desire across her ribs, over her stomach, his hands on the single-button fastening of her shorts even as Fin arched up against him.

A ringing telephone, she learnt at that moment, a *persistently* ringing telephone, could become the most hated object in the world!

Because ring it did. Ring, after ring, after ring, the sound reaching them intrusively from inside the cottage, Jake having left the door open in the heat of the day. Maybe if he hadn't they wouldn't have heard the ringing of the telephone, wouldn't have tried to ignore it—and failed!

'Damn!' Jake rasped savagely as he looked up at Fin regretfully. 'I'll have to go and answer it,' he grated irritably, resentful of the intrusion.

'Yes,' Fin acknowledged with a sigh, her hair a blaze of red against the green of the grass as she still lay back against its coolness.

He got slowly to his feet, running a hand around the back of his neck where it was taut with tension. 'I don't suppose it would be any good my asking you not to move...?' He grimaced even as he made the request.

He knew it was no good, knew the madness of the moment had passed. Just as she did. His gaze lingered regretfully on her nakedness for another second or two and then he turned and walked towards the cottage with determined steps, aggression in every taut line of his body.

Fin didn't relish the chances of the person on the other end of that telephone call getting a polite response from Jake!

She could hear the harshness of his voice from inside the cottage even now as he finally answered the call, getting slowly to her feet, brushing the grass from her clothing. She didn't know whether to be annoyed or grateful herself for the interruption.

If the telephone call hadn't cut in on their passion she didn't doubt for one moment that in a matter of minutes they would have been making love completely. It hadn't been a conscious decision on Fin's part, she just knew it had been inevitable; indeed, her body still ached from that unfulfilled desire. And she was sure Jake hadn't fared much better from the encounter, had felt the throbbing need of his body as he'd lain so close to her.

But ultimately it would have changed nothing, achieved nothing, except to leave her with a yearning ache for something that could never be. Jake would be gone from here in a few weeks' time at the most—she didn't doubt, having come to know him as she did, that he would honour the commitment he had made to directing the play— and she would be left with... What would she be left with? Memories? God, that wasn't enough when she loved him as much as she had realised she did!

He was gone some time answering the telephone call, and Fin could no longer hear his voice, so he must have calmed down too. All of which gave her chance to gather her own scattered defences together. By the time Jake reappeared from the cottage five minutes or so later she could at least give the impression of being back in control—inwardly it was another matter completely!

Jake looked less grim too as he crossed the grass to her side. 'That was David,' he told her lightly. 'Your stepfather,' he enlightened as she still looked up at him in puzzlement.

David; she frowned. What on earth——? 'There's nothing wrong, is there?' she suddenly panicked. 'Mummy——'

'Your mother is fine,' Jake soothed, his expression one of indulgence at her concern. 'No, it seems that David and your mother are arranging a little dinner party for later in the week to celebrate having the baby, and David wanted to invite me to join you all.'

No... Oh, God, *no*!

CHAPTER NINE

WHEN David had first made the suggestion the other evening of Jake's coming to dinner one night Fin had felt herself panic slightly, but Jake's reaction then had been so negative that she hadn't given it another thought. And maybe she should have done, should have said something to David to head off such an invitation, because it was obvious now, from the pleased look on Jake's face, that he had accepted the other man's invitation!

Oh, *God*, she inwardly groaned again. What was she going to do now? What *could* she do?

Jake was watching her with narrowed eyes as he slowly became aware of the fact that she had made no response—no verbal one, at least. It was obvious, as the warmth faded from his expression and his mouth tightened, that he could read plenty from her face. 'You don't want me to go,' he stated flatly.

She swallowed hard at the accusation. 'It isn't a question of wanting——'

'Oh, yes, it is, Fin.' His voice was silkily soft, dangerously so. 'I'm obviously perfectly acceptable to you as a lover no one else knows about, but I'm certainly not to be taken home to "meet Mother"!'

She didn't want him to meet her mother, but that had nothing to do with this. 'You aren't my lover!' she gasped defensively, fiery colour darkening her cheeks.

'If the telephone hadn't rung when it had and interrupted us, I would have been!' He held her gaze, challenging her to deny it if she could.

And Fin knew that she couldn't. Not now. Not any time in the future. She had wanted him as much as he had appeared to want her. Appeared? He *had* wanted her!

'And what would have happened to your relationship with the precious Derek then?' Jake continued scornfully. 'I suppose your mother already *approves* of him!'

As it happened, she had no real idea what her mother thought of Derek, her mother not really ever saying much about him at all. If pushed she would probably say that he seemed 'nice'. Fin frowned at that realisation. She really would have to ask her mother what her opinion of Derek was. At the same time she was sure that Jake wouldn't enjoy being called 'nice' by anyone! And she wasn't sure what her mother would feel about Jake, didn't think she would probably get over the shock of seeing him again enough to express an opinion either way!

'Oh, just go, Fin,' Jake told her impatiently now as she didn't answer his taunt, his expression one of disgust. 'Come back when you stop being little in emotions as well as stature! If I'm still here then I might be willing to listen to what you have to say to me.'

If he was still there, Fin mulled over dejectedly on the drive from the cottage, implying that she could be wrong about that few weeks' grace she had imagined she had, that he might leave very soon after all. And she couldn't bear the thought of him leaving!

It was because she knew she felt that way that she didn't drive straight home. She needed a little longer to come up with a good excuse for David to withdraw his invitation, and also she knew she owed it to Derek, no matter how she might have wavered yesterday, to be honest with him regarding how she felt about him.

She made the drive to Derek's flat with the intention of telling him exactly that. She was more than a little puzzled to find he was still in bed, having hastily pulled on a pair of trousers as he'd hurried to answer the ringing of the doorbell. Fin was more than a little *shocked* when she saw who had been in the bed *with* Derek!

'I can explain,' Derek began to splutter awkwardly as he saw Fin's gaze pass by him to the woman who had followed him from the bedroom, in the act of tying the belt to Derek's robe about *her* waist as she covered her nakedness beneath it.

Sheila. Derek's *secretary*. Although she was obviously more than just that!

Fin had met the other woman half a dozen times or so, had spoken to her on the telephone when she'd called Derek, much more than that. She was ten years older than Derek, married, with two teenage children.

Fin's gaze returned dazedly to Derek; and she had been feeling guilty about the times she had returned Jake's *kisses* . . . !

'Well, what did you expect?' Derek went on the defensive as he saw Fin's astonishment at the whole situation, his face flushed with resentment. 'I told you days ago I wasn't about to sit at home night after night, waiting for you to spare me a few minutes of your time!'

Fin could have pointed out that this was the middle of the afternoon, not 'night', and that what he had just been doing certainly hadn't involved sitting! Well...it might have involved the latter, after all, but she certainly didn't want the details about *that* either.

'I think I had better leave you two alone to talk,' Sheila put in quietly before going back into the bedroom, a tiny, attractive woman with raven-black hair.

Fin didn't think she and Derek had anything left to talk about. They had obviously both been suffering delusions about their relationship—this afternoon should have proved that, to both of them. And now it was over. Because it was over. Even without the involvement of her own confused emotions towards Jake, Fin knew she wouldn't have been able to reconcile herself to Derek's affair with Sheila and just carry on with their own relationship.

Derek glared at her, obviously furious at being caught out in this way. 'You had better come in—— No?' He scowled as she shook her head. 'But we need to talk,' he protested.

She made no effort to step inside the flat, never wanted to do so again, knowing she would always think of him here with Sheila. 'I only came here today to tell you I don't think we should see each other any more. I had intended talking to you,' she admitted. 'But Sheila's presence here makes that rather superfluous.'

'How did you find out about the two of us?' Derek said accusingly. 'Some busybody saw us together, I suppose, and——'

'I had no idea you were involved with Sheila until I arrived here just now,' Fin cut in firmly, knowing she couldn't let him think that was the reason she had come here, to try to catch him out with his mistress!

Although she did wonder now about where he had actually been the other evening when she had telephoned him at the end of that early-finishing rehearsal. Had he been here at the flat all the time, with Sheila, and chosen not to answer the telephone? Could that be why he had been so bad-tempered and defensive the next day? Had the expensive perfume been a salve to his guilty conscience? If it had it certainly hadn't stopped his wanting to continue the affair!

'I don't think it's me you have to worry about any more, Derek,' she told him disgustedly, sure that her conclusions were the correct ones.

He frowned. 'You aren't going to make trouble for me at the office?'

She gave him a pitying glance; was that really all that was important to him, that his job should remain secure? She could see by the resentful flush to his handsome face that it was.

'I was thinking more of Sheila's husband and family, actually,' she said softly. 'But that's for the two of you to work out,' she added flatly. 'Goodbye, Derek.'

'But—look—when will I see you again?' He reached out and clasped her arm.

She was amazed, considering the intimacy of his relationship with Sheila, that he should even want to see *her* again. What was even more amazing was that he should imagine *she* would want to see *him* again after this!

'Never,' she told him with a finality that couldn't be doubted, even by someone as obviously insensitive as him, looking down pointedly at the hold he had of her arm until he slowly released her. 'I'll take my business, such as it is,' she added self-derisively in view of his opinion of her work, 'elsewhere. And don't worry,' she scorned. 'I have no intention of telling your bosses why!' She turned and walked away, her head high, her dignity intact.

Derek and Sheila. Incredible. It had never even occurred to her that Derek would take his resentment towards her other interests, namely the Sovereign Players, and use it to excuse his affair with another woman, moreover a woman who was married to someone else. Thank God she hadn't ever married him, because she had no doubt in her mind now that he would have acted in the same way once they were married if he'd felt the provocation was enough. And what a mess that would have been. The worst of the whole situation was that he didn't even feel guilty over what he had done, considered it was mainly her fault for leaving him to his own devices night after night! She had thought that that was where trust came into a relationship, knew how she had felt today after her own behaviour with Jake. Obviously Derek wasn't troubled by the same sort of loyalty.

She was better off without him, no matter that there didn't seem to be a future for her with the man she *did* love, either!

David was alone in the sitting-room, reading the newspaper, when Fin finally got home, having driven around for a while after leaving Derek, but knowing that she ultimately had to go and at least tell David the truth about Jake; maybe he would know what to do?

'Your mother is lying down,' he told her easily, laying down the newspaper as Fin joined him.

Fin frowned. 'Is she all right?' She had never known her mother to rest during the day before.

'She's lying down on my instructions,' David assured her ruefully. 'Much against her will, I might add,' he added teasingly. 'No, she really is fit and well, Fin. I've spoken to Dr Ambrose myself, without your mother being aware of it, of course,' he grimaced. 'And he says everything is perfectly normal, despite the age thing. The thing is, it's me, really,' he looked a little sheepish. 'I think I'm actually enjoying the role of fussing protector!'

Fin relaxed a little, smiling as she sat down in an armchair. 'I'm sure Mummy is enjoying your *being* like that!'

'She hasn't told me yet what I can do with my fussing,' he acknowledged ruefully, 'so I don't suppose she minds too much. I hope not, be-

cause I have a feeling, as the pregnancy pro-
gresses, that I'm going to get worse!' He winced
self-consciously.

'Mummy will just have to get used to it,' Fin
dismissed distractedly.

David looked at her closely. 'What is it, Fin?
When I telephoned Jake earlier at the cottage he
said you were there with him...' he prompted
softly, his gaze searching.

Her eyes widened at his astuteness in realising
that it was there that her problem lay, but then,
she should have known David would realise there
was something bothering her; he had always been
very sensitive to her problems through adoles-
cence, so there was no reason to think it would be
any different now that she was an adult.

'I was,' she nodded. 'I—um—I was tidying up
for him before Gail gets back tomorrow——'

'You don't owe me any explanation, Fin,'
David said gently. 'I told you I thought Jake was
impressive.'

Fin gave a heavy sigh. 'The problem is, David,
that impressive isn't the only thing he is.' She
chewed on her bottom lip. 'Although he isn't
aware that I know this, Jake Danvers isn't really
his name.' She gave David a pained look.

David frowned, seeming to think this statement over for several seconds. 'I wouldn't jump
to any conclusions because of that,' he finally
said slowly. 'People use an alias more often than

we're, obviously, ever aware. I'm sure Jake has a good reason for using his.'

It was evidence of just how much David liked the other man that he didn't think Jake's behaviour in the least suspicious!

Fin stood up restlessly. 'Oh, he has a good reason for it, David,' she sighed. 'One I know only too well!'

David sat forward in his chair, looking up at her frowningly. 'I'm sure that, whatever it is, Jake isn't a criminal of any kind. I pride myself on being a good judge of character, and——'

'I wish I could be as sure I was,' she told him self-derisively. 'But if you really think you know people that well...tell me your honest opinion of Derek.' She watched him closely.

His brows rose. 'My *honest* opinion?' he challenged. 'Are you sure that's really what you want?'

'Perfectly,' she assured him drily; if he should say anything derogatory about Derek then it couldn't possibly be any worse than what she already thought of him!

David shrugged. 'You asked for it—he's a self-opinionated, selfish, self-centred prig!'

Fin couldn't help her gasp of laughter at his complete candidness.

He raised innocent brows. 'Was that what you wanted to know?'

She nodded. 'I wish someone had told me it earlier—maybe then I wouldn't have had to find it out the hard way!'

David looked at her searchingly. 'And did you?'

'Oh, yes,' she confirmed with finality. 'I won't be seeing *him* again.'

'And Jake Danvers—or whatever his name is?' David probed gently.

'His name is Jacob Dalton,' she told him in a rush. 'Yes,' she confirmed as he gasped. 'I'm sure you know who he is——'

'Angela Ripley's husband...' a voice cut in quietly from across the room.

Fin turned sharply, to see her mother standing in the doorway.

CHAPTER TEN

'YOU'RE sure this is what you want to do?' Fin moved forward as she sat in the back of the car, her mother in the front, seated beside David. 'Jake may not even be at home now——'

'I think we'll just have to take our chances,' her mother told her softly.

Fin had been absolutely amazed at her mother's calmness after being told Jacob Dalton had been living in the area for the last week, that he was, in fact, the new director of *Private Lives*. Instead of being devastated, as Fin had imagined she would be, her mother had been curious to know more about him; what he was like now, what he had been doing with his life for the last ten years. Fin had been expecting almost hysteria, and instead she had found removed curiosity!

'I think,' David had said quietly after Fin's mother had walked in on them earlier, 'the important thing here is what restrictions Fin's knowing Jake's real identity has put on her feelings towards him.' He gave her a probing look.

She had fallen in love with him in spite of those restrictions!

'I thought as much,' David murmured softly when he saw the tears in her eyes. 'Fin, your mother never felt any resentment towards Jacob Dalton. If anything, the two of them shared a pain that could have, if they had had the opportunity to spend any time together at all, formed a bond of friendship.'

She shook her head. 'Mummy has always hated anything that reminded her of Daddy, of the past——'

'Fin, that might have been true once,' her mother cut in gently. 'We all do and say silly things when we're in pain. And I was in a lot of pain when I got back from America after your father died. I destroyed all his photographs, as you know, refused to have his name mentioned around me, but the truth of the matter is, I got over all that years ago. Nine and a half years ago, in fact, when I first met David.' She smiled glowingly at her husband, reaching out to clasp the hand he held out to her. 'I love David very much, Fin. And we're about to have a baby. Nothing, not even the return of Jacob Dalton into my life, and the memories that that naturally evokes, could upset the happiness I have now, with him.'

'But——'

'Not even that, Fin,' her mother repeated firmly. 'It's over. It's in the past.'

And Fin could see that she meant it, every word, that her own worry about the situation had all been in vain, needless. And she had allowed her apprehension about it to interfere with the natural development of her relationship with Jake.

A fact David had been completely aware of, as he'd looked down at her so searchingly, quietly suggesting it was time they all drove over to Rose Cottage and buried the ghosts of the past forever. Her mother had thought it was a wonderful idea, her goodwill towards the whole world at this particular time in her life extending at least as far as Jacob Dalton, and Fin's protests that they couldn't just go there and present themselves to Jake without giving him warning had been to no avail; David and her mother had been adamant.

And so Fin had come with them, all the time wishing herself anywhere *but* here, about to confront Jake with his past in the worst way possible. She doubted that he would take the coincidence of Jenny Halliwell's being her

mother as calmly as her mother seemed to have
accepted his own presence here!

As their car arrived outside the cottage Fin
could see Jake over by the Jaguar, about to get
inside, although he straightened slowly as he recognised David behind the wheel of the car, his
eyes narrowing warily as Fin climbed out of the
back of the vehicle.

His gaze raked over Fin with an expression almost of disappointment, barely registering Jenny's presence there at all, except as Fin's mother
and David's wife.

Fin looked at her mother anxiously, seeing that
she was trembling slightly at seeing this man
again after all these years, despite what she had
said earlier, although she seemed to have her
emotions under control, her expression turning
to one of curiosity now as she realised that Jake
still had no idea who she was. Was she looking
for changes in him? Fin wondered. There had to
be plenty of those, Fin was sure, and not just
physical ones.

'Jake!' David moved to shake the other man's
hand warmly. 'Forgive us for all descending on
you in this way, but once Fin arrived home and
explained things——'

'You decided you had no other choice but to
withdraw your dinner invitation,' Jake finished

scornfully. 'You didn't have to come over here to do that—I was just on my way to see you and tell you the same thing!'

Fin swallowed hard. 'You were?'

He looked at her coldly. 'What other choice did I have?'

'But——'

'Jake,' David put in firmly, 'I would like to introduce you to my wife.' He turned and held out his hand for Jenny to stand at his side, his hand warm as it clasped hers reassuringly. 'Jake, this is Jenny,' he told the other man softly. 'Jenny, this is—— But you know who this is . . . !'

'Hello, Jacob,' she greeted huskily, meeting his gaze steadily as his head jerked up at the correct use of his name rather than the diminutive, frowning at her darkly. 'It's been a long time,' she added ruefully.

Fin watched him anxiously as his gaze moved over her mother searchingly, blankly. And then with dawning comprehension. 'Jenny . . . ?' he voiced doubtfully, as if he didn't believe what his eyes and memory were telling him. 'Jenny *Halliwell*?' He dared to voice the enormity of his thoughts.

'It's McKenzie now,' she corrected with a warm smile. 'But it was once Halliwell,' she acknowledged softly.

He seemed to take a few seconds to take this in, his face very pale when he finally turned to look at Fin. 'Then that makes you ... ?'

'Paul's daughter.' She nodded reluctantly, waiting for the disgust to enter his face—but feeling just as concerned when it didn't. Could it be that he really hadn't known of his wife's affair with her father? This was going to be so much more difficult to explain if he hadn't! 'And you're Jacob Dalton,' she added evenly.

Aqua-coloured eyes narrowed to steely slits. 'Have you known that all the time?'

'Not all the time, no,' she conceded, but at the same time knowing there was no point in not telling him the complete truth now. 'But most of it,' she admitted with a grimace.

His mouth twisted wryly. 'So the joke was on me all the time!' he dismissed self-disgustedly. 'Well, it was very nice of you all to come here and explain just why Fin was so determined that I wasn't going to meet her mother,' he told them briskly. 'But now, if you don't mind——'

'We do mind, Jacob,' Jenny told him firmly. 'We weren't just being nice when we came here.'

'What more do you want from me?' he challenged harshly, his defences up. 'I certainly don't need an audience to witness the fact that I've been behaving like an idiot, talking to Fin in the way I have, confiding my doubts and ambitions to her in a way that I've never——— All this time you've known more about me than I knew!' He glared at her accusingly. 'I feel like a damned fool for even letting you come near me. And how you must have hated listening to me talking about myself!'

'But it wasn't like that!' she protested appealingly. 'I listened to you because I wanted to, because I really thought it helped you to be able to talk to me, because———' She broke off abruptly as she realised she had been about to tell him of the love she felt for him, her cheeks suddenly fiery red. 'I listened because I wanted to,' she repeated softly.

'*Paul Halliwell's* daughter!' Jake burst out frustratedly, as if only now beginning to accept the fact.

'She's my daughter too,' Jenny told him quietly. 'And I believe she cares for you very much.' She looked at Fin with indulgent affection.

'Mummy!' she protested with an embarrassed groan; her humiliation didn't have to be *that* complete.

Jake's expression softened as he saw her agitation. 'I wish———' He sighed deeply, running a hand through the dark thickness of his hair. 'There is so much you don't—*can't* know about what happened ten years ago, things that mean we don't stand a chance as Jacob Dalton and Fin Halliwell.' He looked haggard.

'Things like Paul and Angela's affair, you mean,' Jenny put in softly.

For a moment he looked startled that *she* should know about that, and then he nodded heavily, acknowledging that he had known of it too.

'Like Paul's wanting a divorce so that he and Angela could marry?' Jenny continued ruefully.

The aqua-coloured eyes narrowed. 'He actually asked you for a divorce?'

'Not quite.' Her mouth twisted ruefully. 'I found the letter he had written to me asking for the divorce *after* his death!'

'God . . . !' Jake shook his head disgustedly. 'I thought at least one of us had escaped knowing the truth of their affair all these years.'

Jenny shrugged. 'I knew of it and got over it long ago. And so did Fin,' she added pointedly.

Jake made no reply, and Fin's sense of helplessness deepened. The obstacle that had stood in their way had been removed, and there was still no softening in his attitude towards her. But what had she expected; a declaration of love? It was too much to hope that he felt the same way about her as she did him.

David was watching the other man thoughtfully. 'There's more, isn't there, Jake?' he said slowly. 'What is it we don't know? Just why did you decide to drop out of circulation for ten years? I'm sure you were devastated at the death of your wife, but if you knew of her affair with Halliwell——'

'*Yes*, I was devastated,' Jake bit out gratingly. 'Shocked. Stunned. Finally bewildered and sickened. But not at Angela's death. You see,' he breathed shakily, 'she and Paul weren't the ones who were supposed to perish in that fire—*I* was!' He was almost grey-looking now, lost in the trauma of the memory.

Fin stared at him incredulously, his meaning becoming crystal-clear in the complete silence that followed his statement. The fire hadn't been an accident at all. It had been started deliberately. But it had found the wrong victim—*victims*!

Not her father! She couldn't believe, no matter what else he had done, that he could be capable of such a callous, calculated act.

'Don't look at me like that,' Jake groaned at the distraught expression on her face. 'Paul wasn't involved in it; to his credit he didn't want any part of Angela's plan to get rid of me without the messy publicity that would go along with a divorce between us.' He gave a heavy sigh. 'I overheard them discussing it—arguing about it might be a better description of the conversation. And Paul, for all that he was in love with Angela and wanted to be with her, was shocked at her plotting and scheming.' He gave a disgusted snort. 'I wish I could say I was as shocked, but after three years of being married to her nothing Angela did could really make me feel that way any more!'

'Do you want to start at the beginning?' David said softly, his arm having gone protectively about his wife's shoulders at the first mention of the fire. 'I think, in light of what you have just revealed, that it might be best, don't you?' he prompted evenly.

Jake shrugged defensively. 'I've lived alone with the past for the last ten years; I don't see why I shouldn't continue to do so.'

'And Fin?' David reminded softly. 'What about *your* feelings for her? Because you do care for her, don't you?'

Jake looked across at her with darkly pained eyes. 'Too much to want to inflict the publicity on her that would ensue when it becomes public knowledge that Jacob Dalton is in love with Paul Halliwell's daughter!'

'Jake!' she gasped ecstatically, her eyes bright with love for him as she made a move towards him, only to be stopped in her tracks as he held up his hands defensively. 'Jake...?' She groaned her puzzlement at this further rejection of her; she didn't *care* about the publicity!

He shook his head. 'Loving someone isn't always enough,' he told her grimly.

'But I love you too!' she protested.

'Can't you see that it wouldn't be enough?' he said impatiently. 'I thought it was bad enough when I realised I had fallen in love with a young innocent; now that I know you're also Paul Halliwell's *daughter* the whole thing is ludicrously impossible!'

'As I told you before, Jacob, Fin is *my* daughter too,' Jenny put in firmly. 'And if I know her at all—and I know her very well indeed!—then nothing you have to say will make the slightest bit of difference to the fact that she loves you and wants to be with you! The McKenzie women can be very determinedly single-minded when they have to be,' she added with an affectionate smile at Fin.

'And the McKenzie *man* can vouch for that!' David acknowledged self-derisively, smiling at his wife lovingly.

Fin drew in a deep breath, walking slowly towards Jake, standing just in front of him now. 'Nothing of what you have to tell me has made the slightest difference to my loving you,' she said huskily. 'Does my being Paul's daughter stop you loving me?' She looked up at him anxiously.

'Don't be so damned stupid,' he rasped, much more like the Jake she knew—and still loved! 'You aren't your father.'

'Then——'

'Will you just hear me out?' he cut in harshly. 'See how you feel about me then!'

She shook her head. 'My mother was right, and I've also told you—it won't make any difference.'

'Let's wait and see, shall we?' he said grimly. 'I suggest we all go inside——'

'There's nothing wrong with sitting in the garden, Jake,' David told him lightly. 'Our surroundings aren't going to lessen anything you have to tell us.' He moved through the garden gate, taking Fin's mother with him, sitting down on one of the loungers that still lay there, Jenny at his side.

After an impatient glare in Fin's direction Jake followed the other man with long decisive strides. Fin followed along more slowly, loving Jake so much at that moment, his pain a tangible thing.

And, after keeping the horror of the fire ten years ago to himself all these years, that wasn't surprising! My God, it was unbelievable.

But she did believe him, without question. It seemed incredible that it had happened the way he said it had, that her father and Angela had really intended him to die in the fire, but it explained oh, so clearly why he had been sickened by Hollywood and everything to do with it ten years ago, why he had walked away without hesitation and never looked back.

Until now...

But they could talk about that later; right now she just wanted to be at his side when he relived the pain of the past.

She moved to sit on the grass at his feet, her arm resting across one of his knees as she pressed against him. He shot her a distracted look, obviously deeply disturbed by her proximity, but Fin only returned his gaze with steady intent, having no intention of moving away from him, enjoying just touching him in this way.

A fact Jake seemed to recognise and accept as he began to talk. 'I was only twenty-three when I went to Hollywood, but by the time I was twenty-six I had already directed three successful films——'

'*Very* successful films,' David recalled pointedly.

Jake gave an acknowledging inclination of his head.

'I had seen Angela at the usual parties, heard of her complete professionalism, but the two of us had never actually been introduced. When we finally did meet it was like——' He shook his head at the memory. 'She was beautiful to look at, and her eyes were almost hypnotic, had the ability to make you feel you were the most important person on earth to her.' He gave a shuddering sigh. 'Like dozens of other men before me, I fell for her seemingly unaffected charm. And she seemed to fall in love with me too. We became the Golden Couple of Hollywood.' His face was haggard from the memories.

'When did the "gold" begin to tarnish?' David prompted softly at his prolonged silence.

Jake roused himself with effort, his hand moving instinctively to clasp Fin's as it rested on his knee, unaware that the pressure of his fingers was hurting her. But it was a pain she gladly took for him. 'Almost as soon as we were married,' he sighed heavily. 'Angela liked things her own way, all the time, I discovered, and when they didn't go that way she would lapse into uncontrollable rages. And she would imagine—oh, God, the things she would imagine!'

Fin could imagine that in a place like Hollywood there would be lots of temptation, especially for a man as attractive and powerful as Jake, but she also knew him well enough to know that if he made a commitment to someone then he would honour that commitment; she didn't doubt that he had been faithful to Angela, no matter what his wife might have thought to the contrary.

Jake shook his head. 'She grew up in that artificial world, had been used to having her every whim granted by the film studio; she had no idea how to deal with real life, with real relationships. Marriage was just too real. Especially to me,' he realised ruefully. 'I'm not the lap-dog kind, had my own career to think of, couldn't always be gazing at her adoringly and telling her how wonderful she was, which was what she had been hearing all her life from one source or another. It was what she lived for. After six months of marriage between us I knew we couldn't continue the way we were; the rages were becoming more frequent, the demands ridiculous. But when I mentioned divorce to Angela she swallowed the contents of a bottle of sleeping pills,' he groaned.

Fin looked at him searchingly, only able to guess at the anguish he must have gone through at Angela's attempted suicide. If that was really what it had been? It sounded more to her like the spiteful act of a very spoilt woman who couldn't have her own way, not the cry for help attempted suicide should be.

'Something the film studio hushed up,' Fin's mother said knowingly.

'Of course,' Jake acknowledged grimly. 'She was Angela Ripley, more squeaky-clean than Doris Day! Besides, she hadn't taken enough pills actually to kill herself, only to manipulate her own way,' he grimly confirmed what Fin had already thought. 'And it happened again every time she thought I might be going to raise the question of divorce. She just couldn't bear for anyone to know that our marriage was a failure, a dismal and utter failure; she wanted the whole world to love her. For more than two years I lived with her threats hanging over my head, almost afraid to move for fear that the next time she took the pills it would be the fatal dose.' He made a helpless gesture with his shoulders. 'I couldn't have stood to have her death on my conscience, just because I couldn't love the unbalanced woman I had found her to be.'

'So instead she made you live in another kind of hell.' Fin shook her head dazedly, wondering how he could have lived like that. But what choice had he had?

'I had my work,' he shrugged. 'Kept myself so busy that most of the time I was too tired to even think about the mess my life had become. Angela had a string of lovers by this time, in private; in public she insisted on playing the loving couple everyone expected us to be. I think she actually convinced herself on those occasions that that was exactly what we were, seemed sure, in her own mind, that I did still love her.'

A tragic product of Hollywood, in fact, Fin realised sadly. And it was sad. For Angela. And for Jake.

She smiled up at him lovingly as her fingers tightened about his. All she wanted to do at that moment was put her arms around him and tell him how much she loved him.

He gave her a strained smile in return before continuing. 'I avoided working with her for almost three years,' he sighed. 'But she was the hottest thing in Hollywood, and I—well, the film studio thought it was time the two of us worked together. There was no way I could get out of it, not without telling the whole world why I didn't want to work with her, why just being anywhere near her now made me feel ill. But I needn't have worried.' His mouth twisted self-derisively. 'She took one look at Paul Halliwell and decided she wanted him. And when Angela decided she wanted something—or even *someone*—she usually got it. He—— Oh, God, I'm sorry,' Jake groaned as he realised he was talking about Fin's father now, Jenny's husband. 'If it's any consolation to you, Paul wouldn't have stood a chance once Angela set out to charm him!'

'From what I know of him, he wouldn't have wanted one!' Jenny said drily. 'Although this seems to have been more serious than all the others were,' she added with a frown.

Jake nodded. 'Angela, at long last, seemed to have found someone else she wanted more than keeping our façade of a marriage going, and was ready to let me go. But not in the conventional sense,' he rasped. 'Acting the part of the inconsolable widow, being comforted by her latest co-star, was far preferable to her than having to admit our marriage was a sham, which is what would have happened if it had come to divorce between us. And so she came up with the idea of the fire,' he said grimly. 'After which I would be dead, so no divorce, no messy division of our assets, and no mark against her squeaky-clean image.'

'She was unbalanced,' Fin realised numbly as she thought of the narrow escape he had had.

Jake gave a bitter laugh. 'Oh, yes—definitely. But it all went sadly wrong for her that night,' he recalled grimly. 'From the argument I overheard between the two of them when Paul arrived it was obvious that Angela had been throwing petrol around the downstairs of the house so that the house would go up like an inferno once the fire was started, and Paul, when he realised what she had done, didn't like the idea of the fire one little bit. I had gone upstairs to bed hours before this, but their shouting had disturbed me, and I came out of the bedroom in time to hear most of what was going on.' He shook his head. 'I think I went into shock for a few minutes, hadn't believed even Angela was capable of *that*. In the meantime their argument continued, and when Angela argued she fought like a vicious cat . . . nails, teeth, feet—she hit out with anything that came to hand. Paul seemed as dazed as I was, had obviously never seen Angela in one of these rages before. Everything became a missile—shoes, lamps, ornaments, even the candle she had lit in preparation of starting the fire. Oh, yes,' he confirmed as Jenny gasped. 'She threw that too! The two of them were so busy arguing that they didn't even seem to realise what was happening until it was too late. I tried to warn them,' he said dully. 'But it was too late, they were already trapped. I only managed to get out of the blaze myself by jumping out of the bedroom window. I broke my ankle. Angela and Paul died.'

'Oh, God . . .' Jenny groaned at the horror of it. 'I'm sorry. So very sorry.'

He shook his head. 'I told you, it wasn't Paul's fault. In fact, I believe, I really do, that seeing that side of Angela frightened the hell out of him, and he would ultimately have finished things between them after that night. If he had lived.'

'Thank you,' Jenny told him gratefully, tears in her eyes.

'And what did you do, Jake?' David prompted softly.

Jake roused himself from the past with effort. 'What did I do?' he repeated dully. 'I took myself as far away from Hollywood as possible, tried to forget all of them. I couldn't have succeeded completely,' he acknowledged ruefully, 'otherwise I wouldn't now be in the position of having to decide whether or not I should go back and direct my own screenplay!'

Fin looked up at him still. 'You won't be going alone,' she told him, determined that, no matter what had happened in the past, she was going to spend his future with him. He *loved* her. And she loved him.

He looked pained. 'They would eat you up over there and spit you out again!'

She smiled at him serenely. 'I'm coming with you, Jake.'

'You——'

'I think it's time David and I left the two of you to talk alone.' Fin's mother stood up, holding out her hand for her husband to join her, moving to squeeze Jake's arm reassuringly. 'I'm sorry about what happened to you in the past, but don't let it cloud your judgement where Fin is concerned. Fin isn't Angela, Jake.'

'Thank God!'

'No. I meant——'

'I know what you meant, Jenny,' he drawled, standing up too, pulling Fin up beside him, his arm about her waist as he held her to his side. 'But after ten years of living on my own I'm not sure I—— I never want to hurt Fin,' he added desperately. 'But, as much as I love her and want to be with her, I need to make this film too, need to put the past behind me, once and for all. Maybe when I get back——'

'No,' Fin told him firmly. 'I'm coming with you,' she repeated determinedly.

'But——'

'McKenzie women, Jake,' David reminded ruefully, squeezing the other man's shoulder reassuringly. 'My advice to you is just to give in gracefully; it's much easier on the self-esteem; you're going to lose anyway!'

'Well?' Fin turned to him challengingly once her mother and David had driven away in their car.

'Fin, you don't understand——'

'No, it's you who doesn't understand,' she cut in firmly. 'I love you. I want to be with you. Through the bad times as well as the good. Most of all, I want to be there for you in America.'

His gaze was dark as he looked down at the youthful beauty of her face. 'And what about when they realise you're Paul Halliwell's daughter?'

'They wouldn't have to—not if we were married before we went,' she added almost questioningly, wondering if she was pushing him too far; but she loved this man, wanted to be his wife. 'If we were married, my name would be Dalton,' she pointed out practically. 'Not Halliwell or McKenzie.'

Jake frowned down at her for several seconds, and then the sternness of his features began to relax, finally laughing softly as his arms tightened about her. 'I have a feeling, no matter what your name is, that you're always going to be a McKenzie woman!'

It was going to be all right, she could tell that it was, and she gave herself up to the joy of being kissed by the man she loved and who loved her in return. That was the best part: Jake loved her.

'I thought,' Jake kissed her lingeringly on the lips, 'that you were going to be trouble,' he kissed her again, 'as soon as I woke up that first morning,' and again, 'and you told me you were one of the "little people"!' He kissed her again.

Fin laughed huskily when he raised his head to look down at her. 'I knew *you* were going to be trouble the moment I saw your beautiful naked body and my pulse began to go wild!'

He looked surprised. 'When did you——? So *that's* how you knew to pass me my denims before I got out of bed that morning!' he realised ruefully. 'I *knew* you were going to be trouble when I started talking to you about things I hadn't told anyone else.' He shook his head. 'I never talked about Angela, to anyone, and yet suddenly I did it that day with you. And then I confided in you about the screenplay too.' He frowned. 'I should have realised then that I love you, Fin McKenzie.'

'Er—about the Fin part of my name.' She looked up at him almost shyly. 'It's time *I* told you something no one else here is aware of.' She felt her cheeks grow warm as he looked down at her curiously. 'My actual name is *Elfin*,' she admitted with a grimace.

As Jake looked down at her now it was obvious that he was having difficulty in controlling his laughter. And then finally he couldn't control it any more, letting out a husky chuckle. 'Elfin! My God, no wonder you bristled every time I called you elf or pixie! How on earth did you end up with a name like that?'

'My father thought it would be something unique,' she grimaced.

'Oh, it's definitely that,' Jake agreed, trying to keep a straight face—and failing, grinning openly now.

She shrugged. 'My mother liked the name Fin, and so my father got his way.'

Jake's arms tightened about her. 'Elfin, hm?' he teased. 'I have the ultimate weapon now if *my* McKenzie woman gets too uppity.'

She smiled up at him ruefully. 'I wouldn't count on it!'

'Neither would I,' he accepted indulgently. 'Are you in the mood for a rehearsal?' He quirked dark brows.

Fin frowned. 'But we don't have rehearsals on a Saturday.' Although she was pleased that he intended carrying on with the play, by the sound of it.

He curved her body into his, making her aware of his need. 'I didn't mean that sort of a rehearsal . . . !'

Her expression softened as his meaning became clear. 'There was never any need for a rehearsal between us, Jake; it was always the real thing.'

He sobered. 'I do love you, Fin. Very much, as it happens. And I'll do everything I can to make you happy.'

'I know you will.' She touched his face with gentle fingers. 'But it's a two-way thing. We'll be happy *together*.'

'Look at Daniel,' Fin said indulgently, looking over at the small boy as he peered over the side of the cot that stood in the corner of the large sitting-room.

The three other adults in the room looked at the small child too, Jenny and David like the proud parents they were, Jake anxiously at first until he realised that the year-old Daniel was only curious about the three-week-old baby girl who was his niece. And Jake and Fin's daughter.

What a difference the last eighteen months had made to all their lives. Jake had made his film, a resounding success that had kept them in America for almost a year, although they had both made the trip back when Fin's brother Daniel was born, a healthy full-term baby weighing in at seven pounds nine ounces.

Fin's and Jake's joy had been complete when they had learnt a few months later that they were going to have a baby of their own. Tiny and blonde, like her grandmother, baby Emma was adored from the moment she came into the world with a lusty cry.

Their daughter had been born in England, where Jake was now working on another film, and the three of them lived in a Tudor-style house not far from David and Jenny.

Jake's arm came about Fin's waist now as they looked down at their baby daughter. 'Have I told you today that I love you, Mrs Dalton?' He spoke close to her ear so that only she could hear.

'Oh, yes.' She glowed up at him. 'But I don't mind in the least if you tell me again!'

And he did. Over and over again.

As Fin had predicted, they were happy *together*.

Where do you find hot Texas nights, smooth Texas charm and dangerously sexy cowboys?

THE THUNDER ROLLS
Fireworks—Texas style!

Ken Slattery, foreman at the Double C, is a shy man who knows what he wants. And he wants Nora. But Nora Jones has eyes for only one man in her life—her eight-year-old son. Besides, her ex-husband, Gordon, has threatened to come between her and any man who tries to stake a claim on her. The more strongly Ken and Nora are drawn together, the more violently Gordon reacts—and Gordon is frighteningly unpredictable!

CRYSTAL CREEK reverberates with the exciting rhythm of Texas. Each story features the rugged individuals who live and love in the Lone Star State. And each one ends with the same invitation...

Y'ALL COME BACK...REAL SOON

Don't miss THE THUNDER ROLLS by Bethany Campbell.
Available in October wherever Harlequin books are sold.

Relive the romance...
Harlequin® is proud to bring you

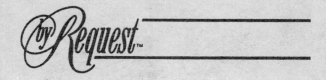

by Request™

A new collection of three complete novels every
month. By the most requested authors, featuring
the most requested themes.

Available in October:

DREAMSCAPE

They're falling under a spell!
But is it love—or magic?

Three complete novels in one special collection:

GHOST OF A CHANCE by Jayne Ann Krentz
BEWITCHING HOUR by Anne Stuart
REMEMBER ME by Bobby Hutchinson

Available wherever Harlequin books are sold.

Calloway Corners

In September, Harlequin is proud to bring readers four involving, romantic stories about the Calloway sisters, set in Calloway Corners, Louisiana. Written by four of Harlequin's most popular and award-winning authors, you'll be enchanted by these sisters and the men they love!

MARIAH by Sandra Canfield
JO by Tracy Hughes
TESS by Katherine Burton
EDEN by Penny Richards

As an added bonus, you can enter a sweepstakes contest to win a trip to Calloway Corners, and meet all four authors. Watch for details in all Calloway Corners books in September.

CAL93

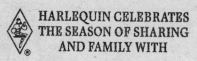

1993 Keepsake

CHRISTMAS

Stories

Capture the spirit and romance of Christmas with KEEPSAKE CHRISTMAS STORIES, a collection of three stories by favorite historical authors. The perfect Christmas gift!

Don't miss these heartwarming stories, available in November wherever Harlequin books are sold:

ONCE UPON A CHRISTMAS by Curtiss Ann Matlock
A FAIRYTALE SEASON by Marianne Willman
TIDINGS OF JOY by Victoria Pade

ADD A TOUCH OF ROMANCE TO YOUR HOLIDAY SEASON WITH KEEPSAKE CHRISTMAS STORIES!

HX93

MEN MADE IN AMERICA

Fifty red-blooded, white-hot, true-blue hunks from every
State in the Union!

Beginning in May, look for MEN MADE IN AMERICA!
Written by some of our most popular authors, these
stories feature fifty of the strongest, sexiest men, each
from a different state in the union!

Two titles available every other month at your favorite
retail outlet.

In September, look for:

DECEPTIONS by Annette Broadrick (California)
STORMWALKER by Dallas Schulze (Colorado)

In November, look for:

STRAIGHT FROM THE HEART by Barbara Delinsky
(Connecticut)
AUTHOR'S CHOICE by Elizabeth August (Delaware)

You won't be able to resist MEN MADE IN AMERICA!

HARLEQUIN PRESENTS®

A Year
DOWN UNDER

In 1993, Harlequin Presents celebrates the land down
under. In October, let us take you to rural New Zealand in
WINTER OF DREAMS by Susan Napier,
Harlequin Presents # 1595.

Olivia Marlow never wants to see Jordan Pendragon
again—their first meeting had been a humiliating
experience. The sexy New Zealander had rejected her
then, but now he seems determined to pursue her. Olivia
knows she must tread carefully—she has something to
hide. But then, it's equally obvious that Jordan has his
own secret....

Share the adventure—and the romance—of
A Year Down Under!

Available this month in
A YEAR DOWN UNDER

AND THEN CAME MORNING
by Daphne Clair
Harlequin Presents # 1586
Available wherever Harlequin books are sold.